A BODY AT THE BOOK FAIR

ELLIE ALEXANDER

Storm

Ebook ISBN: 978-1-80508-991-9
Paperback ISBN: 978-1-80508-992-6

Cover design: Dawn Adams
Cover images: Dawn Adams

Published by Storm Publishing.
For further information, visit:
www.stormpublishing.co

ALSO BY ELLIE ALEXANDER

The Body in the Bookstore

A Murder at the Movies

Death at the Dinner Party

A Holiday Homicide

A Victim at Valentine's

This book is for you! To the supersleuths and armchair detectives —here's to finally solving Scarlet's cold case.

ONE

A warm, sweet spring breeze wafted through the Sitting Room as I managed to force the creaky, old windows open. They'd been sanded, painted, and shellacked so many times over the years that I had to jiggle the brass latch just so and then put my weight into it to let a little fresh air inside. I looked around and drank in the scene as sunlight streamed into the cozy room, hitting the wingback chairs, vintage wallpaper, and tea cart like a spotlight. As the soon-to-be new owner of the Secret Bookcase, I probably shouldn't have favorites when it came to the unique nooks and crannies in our sprawling estate, but I had to admit, the Sitting Room was a pretty delightful spot. The perfect place to curl up with a new read and a view of the English gardens, a cup of rose and strawberry tea in hand.

I stepped away from the windows and tidied the space, making sure the pillows were fluffed and ready for readers. Then I stocked the tea cart with lemon, chamomile, and raspberry-mint tea packets and shortbread cookies. We loved offering little treats and drinks for customers to enjoy while browsing. Next, I wandered to the back of the large, inviting room where collections of our coziest novels—everything in the vein of Miss Marple—lined the bookshelves, and repositioned featured covers so they were facing out. A fire wasn't necessary since June in Northern California was near perfection when it came to the weather, but I lit the electric Mason jar candles and added fresh sprigs of rosemary and lavender to the vases on the mantel. We enjoyed long, luxurious days of sun in Redwood Grove, with naturally cooling gusts from the nearby Pacific Ocean and a bounty of wildflowers blooming in the park and throughout the village square.

If I didn't have a thousand things to do to prepare for my upcoming trip to the California Booksellers Convention (affectionately known in the bookselling world as the CBC), I would have taken a moment to linger and enjoy the stunning view of the climbing roses and wisteria putting on a colorful show in the garden, but as it was, I was already running late. Fletcher Hughes, my coworker and business partner, and I were heading to Santa Clara in a few short hours, and I wanted to make sure everything was in good shape and running smoothly for Hal before we left.

Hal Christie had owned the Secret Bookcase since the early 1980s, when he'd purchased the aging English estate for a song and renovated every square inch, from the ornate Ballroom to the sprawling grounds, transforming it into the largest mystery bookshop on the West Coast. Hal had a serious obsession with Agatha Christie, and was convinced he was her long-lost secret love child. Every room was themed after Ms. Christie, from the Art Deco Parlor, which paid homage to Hercule Poirot, to the Mary Westmacott Nook, where we housed our romance novels, and the Dig Room, which offered our youngest readers an adventure on the banks of the Nile, complete with a sandbox and dinosaur fossils.

I loved working in an immersive and creative space and was committed to maintaining Hal's legacy—not only connecting readers with their next great book. He also believed bookstores were the heart and center of any community, and he welcomed everyone who entered the bookshop with open arms. Fletcher and I were eager to expand on Hal's vision. We had grand plans for more events, festivals, and bookish gatherings.

The convention would be an opportunity to learn from our fellow booksellers and make new industry connections. It was being held at a swanky hotel in Silicon Valley. Over the next four days, I intended to take copious notes and network. I was also planning to spend every spare minute tracking down finite evidence in a cold case murder I'd been working to solve for the last ten years.

In addition to taking over the bookstore, I had recently passed my private detective's exam and was officially a licensed private investigator in the state of California. I still had to pinch myself whenever I opened my wallet and saw my license tucked next to my debit and library cards. Fletcher and I were in the final planning stages of opening Novel Detectives, a private agency we would operate from the bookstore.

It's happening.

It's actually happening.

I did a little happy dance.

This isn't a dream, Annie. It's your new reality.

I practically skipped out of the room but quickly grounded back to earth by reminding myself that there were still plenty of tasks to check off my list before we were ready to open our doors and take on new clients. We needed to adhere to strict rules and regulations to operate within the legal boundaries. Our business permits were filed but not yet approved. We had bank accounts to open, legal contracts to sign, and much more, but there was no denying we were getting close. Opening a private detective agency wasn't a figment of my imagination anymore.

Novel Detectives was a dream that had been a long time in the making. I had studied criminology in college and intended to pursue a career in law enforcement with my best friend, Scarlet. That dream was cut short when she was murdered the day before graduation. Her death sent me into a deep, all-consuming grief. I abandoned any thought of opening my own private agency (something she and I intended to do together) or applying to the FBI or police department. Instead, I found my way to Redwood Grove and wandered into the Secret Bookcase, where Hal had hired me on the spot.

It's not an overstatement to say the bookshop saved me. I surrounded myself with stories and found a new sense of stability and safety with Hal and Fletcher and our amazing community of readers and booklovers. For the last ten years, I'd made Redwood Grove my home, and now everything was coming full circle.

There was one lingering issue—Scarlet's killer. I knew who had murdered her, and I was fairly convinced I knew why, but I needed proof. Definitive proof.

My investigation had shifted as of late. Instead of tracking leads and suspects, now I was singularly focused on bringing Scarlet's killer to justice. Finding tangible evidence linking her killer to the crime had been nearly impossible thus far. But new information had recently come to light thanks to Natalie Thompson, a former employee at Silicon Summit Partners, who was thought to be dead. It turned out that not only was she alive and well, but she had critical information for me—hard evidence linking the killer to the crime. The only problem was that it was up to me to find it. It wasn't a task for the faint of heart, but I'd dedicated my life to solving Scarlet's cold case, and there was no chance I would stop now.

The convention was going to allow me to approach the case differently. It was time for me to step out on my own and face her killer and my past, which had haunted me for too long.

I gulped at the thought and hurried down the hallway toward the Foyer at the front of the historic estate, the boards creaking under my feet. Soft light from the wall sconces guided my way. I drank in the scent of old books and the citrus polish we used on the floors. Being inside the bookshop always felt magical, like I was part of a secret society where everyone who ventured through our doors shared the same passion and devotion to stories.

"Annie, is that you?" Hal peered around the corner between the Conservatory and the Foyer. "I thought I heard someone bustling about, but it's quite early, even for you." He tapped his leather watch strap and crinkled his kind eyes. He was tall with thick white hair and a well-trimmed matching white beard. His face held years of wisdom paired with the best touch of impishness. "Come to think of it, why are you here? Aren't you supposed to be on your way to Santa Clara?"

"Sorry, did I wake you? I came in to get a few things done before we set off. I was trying to be stealthy, but apparently, I didn't succeed." I stood on my tiptoes to kiss him on the cheek and then did a quick survey of the setup. Light flooded into the Foyer through the bay windows. The inviting entry was designed to welcome customers into the bookshop with table displays of new releases, a self-serve coffee and tea station, and plenty of bookish accouterments like stickers, bookmarks, candles, and journals. For spring, we'd decorated with pastel paper flowers and bunches of wildflowers cut fresh from the gardens.

The sandwich board we put outside to welcome readers into the store had a new Agatha Christie quote written in Hal's signature scrawl: I SPECIALIZE IN MURDERS OF QUIET, DOMESTIC INTEREST.

"Don't give it a thought, my dear. I was already up and puttering." He patted my arm and smiled broadly, making the wrinkles in his forehead deepen. "Let me remind you, I can handle the store for a few days. I realize I'm not as nimble or tech-savvy as you and Fletcher, but I won't let you down. You don't need to go to any extra trouble on my account."

"I know." I squeezed his hand gently, appreciating that he was trying to reassure me. It wasn't that I didn't trust Hal. Without him, the Secret Bookcase wouldn't exist. I just didn't want to create extra work for him. He was supposed to be scaling back. "Are you kidding? We're lucky to have you step in. I just feel bad leaving you for the long weekend. My goal is to have everything running like a well-oiled machine, so the only thing you have to do while we're gone is chat with customers about their current favorite reads and ring up sales."

He smoothed his thin cardigan. Hal had a sweater for every season. I often wondered if his closet contained anything other than cardigans and corduroy slacks. For the warm weather promised today, he paired a lightweight sage-green cardigan with a pale yellow T-shirt and khaki slacks. "Believe it or not, I'll manage. It won't be the same without you two, but I am convinced I'll find a way to survive." He flashed me a cheeky grin. "I know my knees are creaky, but don't count this old book-seller out yet."

"Count you out? Never!" I gasped and shook my head. "You've done so much for Fletcher and me. I never want you to think we take that for granted."

"No part of me thinks that. I'm happy to help. To tell you the truth, I'm eager to run the show for the long weekend. I have quite the agenda planned. I've already updated the sandwich board." Hal winked. "Late-night murder parties, plenty of ruckus, enough mayhem to rattle Miss Marple, whatever other havoc I can wreak while you and Fletcher are away."

I laughed. "I'd love to see that."

"Don't you worry. The store will be standing when you return, and I'll hide every last shred of any merrymaking." He shuffled behind the counter and ran his finger over the desk calendar. "It looks like the only weekend event is story time. Our two high school volunteers are leading that, and I see you have already procured snacks, so it seems there's very little for me to do."

I scooted behind him and opened the bottom drawer. "Yes, snacks are here—animal crackers and juice boxes. I bought extra in case we have a large turnout. The past few Saturdays have been a packed house. The volunteers will bring a craft project, and the books are already set up and displayed in the Dig Room."

"See, you're proving my point." Hal threw his hands up in mock helplessness. "The store will run itself. You don't even need me."

I chuckled and shut the drawer. "In all seriousness, is there anything else you need before Fletcher and I take off?"

"Yes. For you to promise me that you'll enjoy the conference and not worry about me or the store." He ran his fingers through his white hair.

"Deal." I grasped the edge of my dress and gave him a playful half bow before smoothing down the whimsical skirt patterned with books. "You're sure you and Caroline are up for watching Professor Plum?" Hal had offered to cat-sit for me. My tabby, Professor Plum, was my best friend and longtime companion. Technically speaking, he was Scarlet's cat, who I adopted after her murder, and leaving him felt like leaving a family member. I knew he'd be in good hands with Hal and Caroline, though.

"Yes, although fair warning, you might not have a cat when you return home. Caroline has purchased toys, treats, and even a special blanket for Professor Plum. She's gone cat crazy. I fear she's using this as a practice run to convince me we need a furry friend."

"You do!" I exclaimed, clapping. "We could have kitten playdates."

Hal stuffed his hands in his cardigan and shook his head like he knew he was outnumbered. "Priya and Liam will be joining you tomorrow. Is that still the plan?" A brief flash of concern crossed his face. "Are you sure it's a wise idea to pursue Scarlet's killer without police support? I realize you all have your roles in your quest to find the documents, but I can't say I'm not worried."

"I know. I'm taking every precaution, and I'll have Pri, Fletcher, and Liam with me. Dr. Caldwell and I have discussed my options at length, and this is the only way." I understood why he was worried. Honestly, I was worried, too, but I had to do this for Scarlet and also for me. I'd tried everything the safe way. Dr. Caldwell had used every available tool and resource. She and her team meticulously combed through Scarlet's case files again. She'd reviewed DNA evidence and old surveillance footage and spent hours re-interviewing key witnesses. She leaned hard on a reluctant informant, hoping they'd crack under pressure, but instead, they clammed up. We'd done a deep dive into the killer's digital trail—texts, emails, financial records—but yielded no incriminating evidence. She'd called in the tech team, but Silicon Summit Partners' defenses were impenetrable. The killer's tracks were expertly covered. The firm's legal team stonewalled us at every turn, citing confidentiality and property protections.

Our failed tactics only emphasized that it was time to step outside of the rules and take a more creative risk. Dr. Caldwell provided me with a solid foundation, both in her coursework and in her recent mentorship. She'd been a sounding board these past few months as I researched everything I could about Silicon Summit Partners and strategized the best approach. Now it was up to me. It was time to get brave and get out in the world.

"You won't take any unnecessary risks, will you?" Hal held my gaze, steadying his eyes on me like he wasn't sure he believed me.

"No, I promise. I've rehearsed my plan a million times and

have at least four different backup plans and exit strategies if it all goes south. I'm not doing this alone, remember? Fletcher is on stakeout, Pri's going to be in constant contact with Dr. Caldwell, and Liam's my muscle." That much was true. They'd all been actively involved in the case and would play a critical role and support in the days ahead. What I didn't say out loud was that while I wasn't going to be *alone*, I was ready to strike out *on my own*. There was an important difference. If I was serious about running Novel Detectives with Fletcher, then Scarlet's murder was my chance to prove I had what it took.

"Good. Good." Hal sounded relieved. He cleared his throat and thumbed through a stack of mail. "I'm glad you're taking Redwood Grove with you."

"Maybe not all of Redwood Grove." I winked. My glasses slipped off the edge of my nose. I pushed them back into place. Although, admittedly, I had packed a bit heavy. I'd tucked all of Scarlet's journals (which I knew pretty much by heart) and my notes and files on her case into my travel bag. I wasn't sure I would need them, but it was better to be overprepared.

"But certainly the best contingent." Hal smiled knowingly and sighed, his voice catching. "I care so deeply for you, Annie. I would be devastated if anything happened to you."

"The feeling is entirely mutual," I replied, pressing both hands over my heart. Hal had become so many things to me over the years—a boss, a mentor, a friend, a surrogate grandfather. His concern was deeply touching. I didn't take for granted what a gift it was to have him in my life. "I won't take any unnecessary risks."

"Excellent. We're on the same page." He set the stack of mail on the counter. "I'm glad that's settled."

"Anything you want us to be on the lookout for at the convention?" I asked, changing the subject. I skirted around him and moved to the front display to adjust the book stacks.

"I trust your eye." Hal swept his hand toward the decorations. "It's like a garden party in here. It's good timing for ordering for the holiday season, though. Before you know it, these paper flowers will be evergreen garlands with holly and mistletoe."

One thing I would never be able to wrap my head around when it came to retail was how early we had to start planning for the holidays. Small, independent bookstores like ours made most of our yearly profits between Thanksgiving and the new year. We had already begun reviewing vendor catalogs for the upcoming season, and my top priority for the CBC was to get a jump start on inventory. "I'm on it," I said to Hal. "It sounds like there are several new reader-based technologies demoing their products at the show. I'll be eager to see what's coming on the market."

"I'll leave that to you and Fletcher. You know what a Luddite I am. Give me a rotary phone and vintage typewriter any day." Hal pretended to place a rotary call, circling his finger clockwise.

I laughed. "So you say, but I've seen how addicted you are to your morning mind games, as you call them."

Hal's eyebrows lifted. He pressed his fingers to his lips. "Shhh, that's supposed to be our little secret."

"My lips are sealed." I pretended to zip my mouth shut.

"On that note, I'll pour myself a cuppa and find a spot in the Conservatory to finish my morning mind work before it's time to open."

I left him to his crosswords and puzzles. I checked my phone and saw that Fletcher had texted to let me know he was grabbing us coffees at Cryptic and would be at the store shortly. That gave me time to complete my walk-through and gather my things. In an hour or so, we would be in Santa Clara, surrounded by our book friends and within striking distance of Scarlet's killer. I bit my lip as I ran through the plan for how I would force a confession. Would it work? I didn't know, but I believed in my skills and ability. If it didn't work, I had another ace up my sleeve—intel about secret files hidden somewhere within the building. Where? That was the problem. I had no idea, but I would figure it out once I was inside Silicon Summit Partners headquarters. I didn't have another choice—I just had to get in there, and then I would find a way.

TWO

Fletcher arrived balancing a tray of coffee in one hand and dragging a suitcase with the other. Neat tracks in the pea gravel path marked his route from the village square to the bookstore. He was tall and gangly with a long, angular face and sharp jawline. "I'm road trip ready," he said, offering me the coffee. "Pri said this is a seasonal Annie special to get you in the book-convention mode. It's a strawberry-almond latte with a touch of rose water and an extra shot for courage."

"That should do it." I took the coffee from him, breathing in the intoxicating aroma of the rich brew and the sweet smell of jasmine wafting in with him. "An extra shot never hurts."

"The London Fog is for Hal." Fletcher propped his hound-stooth suitcase by the front door and stretched one arm out so I could see his outfit. "What do you think? Does it scream Sher-lock? Is it on-brand for the Secret Bookcase? Don't say it's too much because the brochure clearly stated costumes are highly encouraged."

"Far be it from me to rain on your parade, Mr. Holmes." I studied his outfit—er—costume—uniform? For Fletcher Hughes, it was typical daily wear. However, he tended to tone down his penchant for deerstalker caps and pipes while on duty at the bookstore. For our excursion to the CBC, he had opted for a more modern take on Sir Arthur Conan Doyle's cunning detective. He looked like he was auditioning for the part of Benedict Cumberbatch's body double with his long black trench coat, black slacks, and navy scarf. "Aren't you going to be hot?" I pointed outside to the cloudless blue sky.

"The convention is *inside* a hotel, Annie. I have it on good authority that the air conditioning will be running on high. I went straight to the source for that intel." He waved me off with a dismissive flick of his wrist. "But not to worry, my dear Watson, I can peel off layers as I go, and I tucked a magnifying glass and a calabash pipe into my suitcase just in case." He tapped the side of his long, narrow cheek with a finger and gave me a conspiratorial nod.

I shook my head and rolled my eyes. "What am I going to do with you?"

"Tough to say because you're stuck with me. We've already signed the contract, so there's no turning back now."

I was happy to be "stuck" with Fletcher. Our skill sets complemented one another, and he had become like a brother to me. Fletcher was detail-orientated to a fault—a kindred spirit when it came to data and spreadsheets. He could lose himself for hours following every thread and going down every rabbit hole during research. Facts were his comfort zone. He preferred to let me be the face of our investigations.

"I'm impressed with the book dress, Annie," Fletcher continued, removing the lid from his coffee and blowing on it. "You know it's a gateway dress, though. Watch out; it's a slippery slope. You'll be sporting a full Miss Marple outfit before you know it."

"Never." I shot him my best intimidating scowl and sipped the latte. The rich, velvety flavor hit my tongue, practically making my tastebuds sing with delight. Priya Kapoor, or Pri to those who knew and loved her, was an absolute genius at crafting gorgeous, nuanced, layered coffee drinks. The latte was no exception. It was slightly sweet and fruity from the strawberries with a nutty, floral finish. She had managed to strike the perfect balance with the rose water. Too much, and the coffee would taste like my grandmother's perfume. Not enough, and the flavor wouldn't come through. But it was there, at the back of my tongue, lingering like a sweet kiss.

"Pri told me to pass on that she and Liam are carpooling and will get in later this evening. They want to meet for a drink in the hotel lobby to strategize." Fletcher secured the lid again and took a timid sip like he was worried he might burn his tongue.

"Sounds good." I took another long drink of the coffee, savoring the latte and the fact that I was so lucky to have such an amazing and supportive group of friends. It helped bolster my courage. I was going to need every ounce of it in the days ahead.

"Do I smell Cryptic?" Hal cleared his throat as he entered the Foyer.

"One London Fog at your service." Fletcher gave him a half bow and handed him the cup.

"Why are you two dallying? Shouldn't you be on your way by now?" Hal's eyes drifted to the typewriter clock on the wall behind the cash register.

"Fair point." Fletcher picked up his suitcase. "I'm ready. Annie, you?"

"Let's do it." I hugged Hal, grabbed my coffee, and retrieved my bag from the hall closet.

Hal came onto the porch and watched us go, waving like a parent sending his kids off to college. "Have fun! Order a lot of books and say hello to everyone for me!"

We walked down the long gravel lane to Fletcher's car. The grounds looked as if they had been painted by one of the impressionists. Emerald-green grasses and dark mossy topiaries provided a lush landscape in the English garden, where dozens of varieties of native Californian wildflowers burst in bright pops of color. Water gurgled in ornate fountains. Our resident crows, Jekyll and Hyde, circled overhead as if escorting us to the car like our own personal bodyguards.

Fletcher had trained the crows to bring him trinkets in exchange for peanuts. Not a day went by when I didn't find a shiny penny or pebble on the Terrace or waiting for me at the front door. Jekyll and Hyde had quickly become our unofficial mascots, especially after they'd watched over me and alerted me to danger earlier in the year.

"Keep an eye on Hal," Fletcher hollered to the crows. They grazed over our heads, cawing in agreement as they peeled off and flew toward the park.

The estate was bathed in a golden, sepia-toned glow. Ancient ivy and wisteria snaked toward the roofline, gripping the stucco in an enchanting embrace. Pink and green bunting stretched from the house to the opposite side of the pathway. It was Hal's signature welcome. As an Anglophile, he wanted everyone who visited the Secret Bookcase to feel like they were stepping into a quaint village in the English countryside.

"My car is this way." Fletcher pointed to Cedar Avenue as we arrived at the end of the lane. He offered to drive since I'd be returning home with Liam, and Fletcher intended to stay an extra night to see his new paramour, Victoria. They met at a matchmaking event we hosted at the bookstore in February. Things were still relatively fresh with Victoria. She worked for Book Emporium, a large big-box store, but she had recently ventured out on her own to start a bookmobile that serviced rural areas and communities without a local bookstore—the Book Bus.

"Thanks for driving." I followed him to the car and helped load our bags in the back.

"No problem. I enjoy the road. The twists and turns

through the coastal mountains always make me feel like a Formula One racer at the Monaco Grand Prix."

"I hope you're not planning to drive that fast." I buckled my seatbelt tighter.

"I'm teasing. You know what a rule follower I am." Fletcher set his coffee in the console and steered the car past Oceanside Park. The park was the crown jewel of the village square, encircled by majestic redwoods, leafy oaks, and the fresh, almost minty aroma of eucalyptus trees. A network of winding trails cut through the grassy areas to secluded picnic spots, children's play areas, and an outdoor amphitheater.

"I figured we might use the time to review the case," Fletcher said. "And finalize your plan of attack for the hundredth time."

"*The* case?" I raised my eyebrows. "Really? Again?"

"If you're up for it." He kept his eyes on the road. "It might be good to review everything we've learned thus far. Once we get to the convention, we won't have much extra time. It's probably going to be sensory overload, and you simply cannot be overprepared for this, Annie. Your life depends on it—literally."

"Yeah. You're right." I watched the redwood trees lit by the sun, their towering trunks rising to the sky. They remained rugged and steadfast, holding the weight of countless seasons. If the trees could weather the raging storms that blew in off the Pacific Ocean, I could weather what was coming next. These giants had remained rooted for centuries, longer than I'd been alive. There was something deeply reassuring about their stillness, like I could almost reach out and harness their power. Truth be told, I needed every ounce of power possible.

"Okay, let's start from the beginning. Consider me your sounding board." Fletcher kept a tight grip on the wheel.

I sighed and closed my eyes briefly. "We know Scarlet was meeting Bob, her source, on the day she was killed," I said, repeating information that I knew as well as I knew myself.

"Scarlet believed she had a break in the cold case we were investigating. We were all convinced that Natalie Thompson, our subject, was murdered because of what she uncovered about Silicon Summit Partners."

"Yet now we know she's alive and well," Fletcher added.

"Exactly. This is why I'm leaning toward believing that Scarlet must have realized that. She was unstoppable. Those files she hid in Professor Plum's collar—she was doing her due diligence, gathering evidence, building her case against the firm." In the past year, I'd had several breaks. First, the discovery of the documents saved on a computer chip stashed in Professor Plum's collar; then a meeting with Mark, a former employee; and finally, a letter from Natalie explaining her involvement with Silicon Summit Partners, revealing that she'd basically been in hiding for the last decade.

Dr. Caldwell had assigned Natalie's case to our class. Natalie had been presumed dead. Scarlet and I spent every waking minute looking into leads. Natalie worked as Logan Ashford's executive assistant. He was the CEO of the brokerage firm. In our research, we uncovered her personnel files. She'd received glowing reviews and quick promotions in her first few years in the position, but something shifted. She became withdrawn and paranoid. Her family and friends were worried about her. Rightfully so.

Natalie went to the police with claims that Silicon Summit Partners was involved in a corruption scam involving high-ranking political figures. The police dismissed her, labeling her a "woman scorned." They pegged her as having an affair with Logan that ended poorly and assumed she was trying to exact her revenge. Only she ended up missing days later and was presumed dead.

"I keep coming back to Mark," I said to Fletcher, watching a dizzying symphony of colors flash by the window. Swaths of coral, orange, and pale yellow poppies created fields of gold along the side of the road. "I think Mark is 'Bob,' Scarlet's source. It's the only thing that makes sense. When he met me in December, he was too smooth. Too casual. I'm convinced he knew more than he let on and was trying to get a sense of how much I know and report his findings to Logan."

"And there's the Tesla issue." Fletcher flipped on his blinker and turned onto the two-lane highway. "We're here. Right at the scene of the crime. What uncanny timing."

I shuddered at the memory. The day I met Mark, I was walking on the side of the tree-lined road when a white Tesla tried to run me down. Fortunately, I'd jumped into a ditch at the last minute. I ended up with some bumps and bruises, but it could have been much worse. At dinner that night, Mark let it slip that he rented a Tesla. It fit with his tech-bro vibe. The police were never able to find the car. In part because I dove to safety before I had a chance to get a glimpse of a license plate.

Mark had been the person who had let me know that Natalie was alive. He also showed me the employment contract Scarlet had signed with Logan Ashford. I'd been so grateful for information that I let my guard down. It was a rookie mistake and something I wouldn't let happen again.

"And you think Mark is doing Logan's dirty work for him?" Fletcher asked, already knowing what my answer would be. We'd been over this too many times to count. Although, I had to admit it was lovely that we had such a mind meld; it felt like a clear sign that our partnership was meant to be.

"Yes—that must be the explanation, right? The pictures Natalie sent me of Mark and Logan posing and looking so chummy together validate that. I think Mark and Logan wanted me to know about Natalie—hoping maybe if I knew she was alive, I'd finally stop digging. When I didn't, they tried again with Elspeth." I stared out the window again, watching the highway twist and turn in the distance. Beams of sun slanted through the trees like a spotlight. I'd had two recent brushes with death. First, the Tesla, and then I was pushed off a cliff by another woman, Elspeth. She was hired by whoever wanted to stop me from pursuing the investigation. She'd been arrested but refused to give up a name despite Dr. Caldwell's offers of a reduced sentence in exchange for her testimony—yet another dead end.

"All right, so no matter what we discover, we keep coming back to Mark and Logan around every new nugget of information or single clue." Fletcher's tone was even and calm. I appreciated his ability to keep his emotions in check. I had been so emotionally tethered to Scarlet that separating my deductive abilities and internal rage had been challenging, but not anymore.

I nodded, shifting my gaze back to him. "Dr. Caldwell used to tell us not to overthink a case, that sometimes the most logical explanation was the correct explanation."

"Exactly. The looming question is, how do you get the proof?" Fletcher's grip tightened on the wheel. "We can operate slightly differently than the police as the Novel Detectives. I'm nervous about the document I created. What if Logan doesn't believe it? Or what if he won't meet with you?"

"He will," I said with confidence. I had been a thorn in Logan's side for months, calling, emailing, and sliding into his DMs, asking relentless questions about Scarlet. Fletcher had spent the better part of the last month writing up a twenty-five-page risk analysis report of Silicon Summit Partners' security protocols. Some of it was forged, and some of it was based on actual data. It was my ticket in the door, and I had complete faith in Fletcher. His painstaking, meticulous work left no room for interpretation.

"I hope you're right." He didn't sound like he shared my conviction in his skills. I noticed how his Adam's apple bobbed as he swallowed and how the tips of his fingers were turning white from his death grip on the steering wheel. "I'm here to follow your lead. I just wish I could come up with a better, fool-proof plan. This is where we could really use a Sherlock Holmes in our life."

I punched him gently in the arm. "Hey, I've got a Fletcher Hughes. I don't need a Sherlock."

He scowled, keeping his eyes planted on the highway. "I hate to sound like Hal here, but your plan is dangerous, Annie. Do you actually think you can pull this off? And what are the odds that the evidence Natalie stashed at Silicon Summit Partners is still there? Not to mention, what if you can't find it?" His voice cracked slightly.

I bit the inside of my cheek and shook my head, letting my gaze drift to the changing scenery again as we ascended through the mountains. The coastal forest stretched as far as I could see in a shimmering carpet of green.

I let out a long sigh, considering Fletcher's question. I didn't know how I was going to accomplish the weighty task, but I had faith an answer would reveal itself. I just hoped that would happen sooner rather than later. For the time being, my only play was me. I'd explored every other possibility. I also knew when I told everyone we were moving ahead with Operation Silicon Summit, they weren't going to like it.

I wished there was another way or that we could count on the authorities, but they were in bed with Silicon Summit Partners.

We were on our own.

More specifically, I was on my own.

Over the last few months, in countless conversations with Natalie, I'd pieced together a startling revelation—she had stashed critical evidence on the Silicon Summit Partners campus. She recounted the tense weeks leading up to her departure when her paranoia became almost unbearable. I could hear the fear in her voice when she told me how she felt like the walls were closing in. She couldn't handle the weight of knowing the police were unwilling—or unable—to help, so she made a bold and dangerous decision to take matters into her own hands.

Natalie had quietly gathered and copied sensitive documents linking Logan Ashford to a web of crimes—fraud, bribery, and assault. The documents were all carefully preserved in a cache she'd hidden away.

I nearly passed out when she told me. It was like a gift from the gods—hard, damning evidence with Logan's name plastered everywhere. But my excitement faded when the trembling and trepidation in Natalie's voice grew stronger as she explained that she had no idea if the evidence was still in the building. She believed Scarlet had found her documents, and that's what ultimately got her killed. "Be careful. Logan is a monster."

I thanked her profusely and started crafting my plan the minute we hung up.

Logan Ashford might believe he was all-powerful and untouchable.

But I had one trick left up my sleeve—me. I would offer myself as bait.

Did it mean putting myself in danger?

Yes.

Did I care?

Not exactly.

"Annie, you got quiet," Fletcher said, taking his eyes off the road briefly and glancing at me with concern. "Are you okay? I'm not trying to put pressure on you. We can wing it. That's what we've done in the past, and look how it's turned out."

"Yeah, right. I'm good." I smiled. "I'm just ready to get this over with and do whatever it takes to put Scarlet's killer behind bars for good."

THREE

We arrived in Santa Clara and found our way to the hotel. It was a two-story midcentury modern building flanked by palm trees and retro pink flamingos. The center courtyard boasted an aquamarine swimming pool with bright yellow lounge chairs and navy-and-white-striped cabanas. The lobby looked like a set from a retro sitcom. Funky chairs in tangerine and teal with geometric throw pillows were arranged around a gold bar cart stocked with fancy bottles of gin and bitters for happy hour. Glass cluster chandeliers gave the room a dazzling light. Gold accents were everywhere.

"This is cool," Fletcher said. "Quintessentially California."

"And the complete opposite aesthetic of the Secret Bookcase." I laughed, motioning to our attire—my book dress and his Sherlock garb.

"Are you here for the book conference?" a young staff member asked as we approached check-in.

"What gave us away?" Fletcher asked, tossing his scarf over his shoulder with a flourish.

"We don't get a lot of scarves and trench coats in June," the staff member replied with a chuckle. "It's supposed to be near eighty this afternoon." She glanced at me. "The book dress is another clue. Cute, by the way."

"Thanks." I grinned at her and elbowed Fletcher in the stomach. "Told you so."

"Not at all. We have a budding young detective on our hands, Annie," he said, addressing the woman. "We should recruit you for our detective agency." Fletcher reached into his pocket and passed her a Novel Detectives business card. Pri helped us design the logo—a silhouette of two crows (inspired by Jekyll and Hyde) studying a magnifying glass with the words Novel Detectives written in cursive. "I'm serious. We're hiring; if you ever want to put your deductive skills to work, or if you need to hire our services for any reason, give us a call. We're the Novel Detectives in Redwood Grove."

"Where's Redwood Grove?" The employee flipped the business card over.

"It's a small town about thirty minutes from here. Almost to the coast, but not quite," Fletcher replied, starting to launch into specific directions. "You can take two different routes."

I jumped in. Otherwise, Fletcher might talk her ear off for the next hour about the pros and cons of driving north toward San Francisco or south toward San Jose, and I didn't want to miss the opening session. He had a penchant for sharing—or oversharing—his eclectic knowledge base, whether useful or not. "Do we check in with you for the convention?"

"No. I'll take care of your rooms. Once you drop off your bags, go to the theater. There's another large lobby with check-in for the event. You can't miss it—balloons, banners. It looks like a book carnival." She pointed out the conference area on a paper map and gave us our keys.

We stepped away from the desk and studied the map.

"Meet you at the theater in five minutes?" Fletcher said, already dragging his bag to the elevator.

"Sounds good." I nodded and headed for the stairs. I found

my room on the second floor. It was styled like the rest of the hotel with midcentury touches. There was a small sitting room attached to the bedroom and a coffee bar filled with treats and various local coffee blends. Pri would appreciate that, I thought, as I opened the shutter doors that led to a small private balcony and a view of the pool. The shimmering oasis called to me. The turquoise waters glinted in the sun, surrounded by a wide deck paved with tiles. Lounge chairs and cabanas with bold striped cushions lined the deck. Lush palms waved in the warm breeze. While I would miss my cozy hometown for the next few days, I could get used to this.

I was tempted to reserve one of the cabanas and spend an afternoon curled up in the warmth of the early summer sun with a book and an ice-cold lemonade, but there was so much to do—another time.

"Liam and I can have our coffee outside overlooking the pool and palms tomorrow," I said aloud to no one as I unpacked. I'd always had a habit of talking to myself. My inner monologue never stopped, which was both a blessing and a curse. I carefully organized Scarlet's journals and my notes in the nightstand, my fingers lingering on the worn pages. For what felt like the hundredth time, I flipped through them, drawn into her intricate designs and sketches. Her artistry came through in her drawings and puzzles—keys without locks, mazes without exits, and cryptic phrases. Scarlet hadn't just loved puzzles; she'd lived them, and now I had to figure out how to piece this last one together.

I sighed and put the journal away. Then I quickly checked my appearance in the oval bathroom mirror. My reddish curls fell softly to my shoulders. I pinched my cheeks to give them some extra color and made sure my glasses were straight. The blues in my dress brought out the golden flecks in my eyes.

Satisfied I was presentable for the conference, I returned to the main floor to meet Fletcher. As the receptionist had mentioned, it was impossible to miss the convention. The lobby was filled with special book décor—vintage typewriters and parchments with ink and quill pens. A cozy book nook had been set up in a corner of the bar with oversized armchairs, couches, and stacks of books tied with satin ribbons. The bar was transformed for the weekend with signage touting special literary-themed drinks like One Flew Over the Cosmo's Nest, Murder on the Orient Espresso, and Gin Eyre. Temporary bookshelves flanking each side of the retro bar housed a lending library with a title for every booklover.

We're having drinks there later, for sure.

I continued to the back half of the property to the convention space and theater, which opened onto the grassy areas next to the pool, bringing the outdoors inside. It was lovely to have fresh air and natural breezes, especially since we'd be in sessions throughout the weekend. Book bunting and twinkle lights were strung across the ceiling. A giant balloon arch greeted me, along with sculptures and artwork crafted entirely from books. Everything smelled like tropical sunscreen, chlorine, and books—the perfect combination in my mind.

Fletcher was in line to check in. I scooted next to him. "This is incredible." I pointed to the dainty paper butterflies dangling from the ceiling. Discarded pages of literary works had been folded like origami and transformed into a magical display of art.

"Plus, we get merch." Fletcher ran his hand along his book tote like he was in a fashion show.

"You're just in time. The opening session is starting now, but you should hurry." A volunteer gave us our badges and directed us to a few remaining empty seats in the last row of the theater. Like the rest of the hotel, the theater was modern, with tiered seating, bright lighting, a large, teak stage, and a state-of-the-art sound system. Book banners hung from the arched ceiling, and stunning flower arrangements—pink and white roses crafted from the pages of old books—were elegantly arranged along the edge of the stage. A long table, draped with a linen tablecloth, sat in the center of the stage awaiting panelists.

It was impossible not to be impressed with the detailed touches. The organizers had gone to great lengths to make us feel like we had stepped into a spellbinding and bewitching book world.

"Welcome to the future of bookselling, everyone." A man jumped on the stage and grabbed the microphone. He was about my age, probably in his early to mid-thirties, with a well-trimmed goatee and a thrifted wardrobe. "I doubt I need an introduction, but in case you're not familiar with the future—and trust me, you should be because it's not coming, it's already here—I'm Fox Andrews."

"That's Fox Andrews?" Fletcher whispered. "I pictured him much younger."

"Me too." Fox Andrews had made headlines in nearly every trade magazine for his new technology. He was a self-proclaimed wunderkind on a mission to revolutionize and completely digitize the reading experience. His invention, the Headset, claimed to "step the readers into the story" with a fully immersive VR experience. He'd been featured in every bookselling magazine lately. The Headset was touted as revolutionary and the best thing to come along since the invention of e-books and e-readers.

"I know you're all here because you want to see and demo the Headset." He glanced to the side of the stage and whispered something to whoever was standing in the wings. "I've got it tucked away, safe and sound. You will have a chance to see it in action. Be sure to come to my panel at one o'clock this afternoon. But before we get to that, the organizers have asked me to introduce you to an author who, like me, needs no introduction."

"He's so humble, isn't he?" Fletcher teased with a roll of his eyes.

"I wonder who the author is." I leafed through the program. Several bestselling authors were attending the convention. That was one of the selling points for attendees. Publishers sent hundreds of copies of books for their featured authors to sign and give away. It was the perfect opportunity to get new titles in front of every bookseller in the state and a great way for booksellers like us to connect with authors and invite them to our stores for signings and special events.

"He's making it sound like a surprise bonus author." Fletcher rubbed his hands together in eager anticipation, rounding his lips and letting out a little whistle. "What if it's someone from Arthur Conan Doyle's estate?"

"Don't get your hopes up." I didn't want to break it to him that today's readers and booksellers probably wouldn't consider someone from Arthur Conan Doyle's estate a big name.

Fox glanced to the side of the stage again and gave a half nod as if confirming that the author was ready for their big reveal. "Guys, gals, and nonbinary pals, the moment you've all been waiting for—let's give it up for the one and only, all the way from London, Serena Highbourn." His voice boomed as he stretched out her name like a sports announcer hyping a star player.

Oohs and aahs erupted from the crowd, followed by thunderous applause as Serena Highbourn took the stage.

"Serena Highbourn? No chance. How did they land her? I heard she wasn't doing appearances any longer." Fletcher jumped to his feet, clapping with enthusiasm as a short, petite woman in her late fifties with long, glossy white hair and giant beetle-like black glasses strolled casually to center stage.

"Serena, welcome to California." Fox swept his hand toward the audience. "It sounds like our booksellers might be familiar with your backlist."

Serena snatched the microphone from his hand and practically hip-checked him. Fox stumbled but recovered quickly, giving her a bow and ducking off the stage with a wave and a reminder to come to his panel. Serena was unimpressed. I'd heard that she was a bit of a diva. She wrote a trove of scandalous, juicy celebrity tell-alls. No one had any idea how Serena Highbourn convinced her sources to bare their souls to her, but they did. Again and again, leading to numerous bestsellers that sold millions of copies.

She got dirt and gossip long before anyone else. Dozens of theories abounded as to how she garnered insider info on celebrities, dignitaries, and politicians, but whatever her tactics, she kept them and her sources under tight wraps.

The preorder rush for any of her books was a literal mob scene. Fortunately for us, Serena was passionate about supporting indie bookstores, so every release brought in a flux of new cash and customers.

"Yeah, I reached out to her publicist a while ago, and she told me Serena was on an indefinite touring break," I said over the screaming. People were on their feet, giving her a standing ovation.

Serena's books weren't my thing. I barely followed celebrity news or gossip. But at the Secret Bookcase, a mystery-inspired shop, we always had a line out the door whenever she released a new title. For someone of her status to demand preorders and signed copies would only be sold at indie bookshops was huge. She could have partnered with a big-box store for an exclusive edition and probably doubled her advance, so even though pop-culture scandals weren't my go-to reads, I appreciated her devotion to small shops and the revenue and customers it brought in.

"Thank you. Thank you." She tapped the top of the mic and motioned for everyone to sit. "I'm grateful for your generous welcome."

"We love you, Serena," someone nearby shouted.

"I know. Thank you." She raised a hand to quiet the crowd. "I'm thrilled to be at the California Booksellers Convention, and I want you to be the first to hear it." She paused for effect. People chattered with eager anticipation. "I just delivered my new manuscript to my editor, and I'll be reading an exclusive first chapter this weekend."

The audience responded like we were at a rock concert.

Fletcher joined in the excitement, clapping and whooping again. I couldn't take my eyes off Serena. She should have been savoring the moment with hundreds of her adoring fans and booksellers who would hand-sell her new book and no doubt make it another instant bestseller. Instead, her gaze was locked on Fox Andrews. He stood in the front row, staring back at her and dangling the Headset like a hypnotist lulling their subject into a trance.

What he did next gave me pause.

He looped the Headset over his eyes and fired off a round of fake gunshots aimed directly at Serena with his thumbs and forefingers.

She flicked her hand and returned her attention to the audience. I had no idea what their connection was, but it was clear that something was going on, and there was deep-seated animosity between them.

FOUR

The theater buzzed after Serena concluded her announcement.

"Wow," Fletcher said, turning towards me. "We're already off to a banging start. I had no idea we'd get a surprise appearance by Serena Highbourn. How do you think she does it? Blackmail? I wonder if she has a team of spies who are on constant celebrity stakeouts. Like her own Baker Street Irregulars." Fletcher shook the thought away and studied the program, running his finger along the event lineup for the day. "What do you want to do? Should we divide and conquer? I'm interested in the panel on merchandising. What about you?"

"I'm curious about Fox's panel." I reached into the tote bag we'd received as part of our ticket for a pen. It included a program, a water bottle, a notebook, a pen, and a schedule of all the events, signings, and panels. I began circling the key events I was interested in attending.

"Can you imagine Hal selling customers the Headset?" Fletcher laughed, pointing to a glossy ad in the program for Fox's new product. "I'll be eager to hear your thoughts on the demo. He claims the VR is so good you'll feel like you're inside the pages of your favorite novel. Although, I certainly wouldn't mind a virtual visit to 221B Baker Street."

"It's a bold claim, but if he can really create fictional worlds like he says, I can see a market for that."

"Supposedly, publishers are scrambling to be a part of it." Fletcher looped his tote over his arm. "If it lives up to the hype, it very well may revolutionize how we read."

"I'll report back." I gathered my things and headed for one of the small conference rooms. The first panel I wanted to attend was a talk about how indie shops could build community. Like the rest of the convention space, the smaller breakout room was decked out in book décor—more of the paper book flowers and book bunting gave the stage a welcoming feel. I found a seat next to an older woman in her seventies. "Is this spot taken?"

"No, please. Sit." She looked flustered as she gathered four different tote bags from the seat to make room for me. Her assorted totes were embroidered and stamped with book quotes and pretty artwork. Each was stuffed with books and trinkets to the point they were bulging like Santa's overflowing sack. Stickers, bookmarks, and plush blankets rolled tight with ribbons practically spilled out from the top of each tote. "I'm Laurel Deters," she said, stuffing a cashmere book scarf back into one of the bags.

"Nice to meet you. Annie Murray, Secret Bookcase," I said, taking a seat.

"Oh, yes. Of course. Yes. I've heard of your store. Everyone knows about it. You're like book royalty. It's a mystery shop. Agatha Christie themed, is that correct?"

"That's us." I nodded with a warm smile. It was always a treat to hear that people were familiar with the bookstore. "What about you? I see from your name tag you're also a bookseller."

She reached for her badge and stared at it like she was

surprised to see her name. "Yes, well, this is all new to me. I opened my shop three months ago. It's been a lifelong dream. My husband, Albert, died last spring, and unbeknownst to me, he left me a bookstore nest egg in his will. It was his final gift and last surprise. He was like that. He loved to plan secret getaways. We used to imagine owning our own little bookshop. We were married for nearly fifty years, and he still found a way to surprise me after his death. Can you believe it?"

"That's so romantic." I placed my hand over my heart, feeling a swell of emotions. What a sweet gesture from her husband and a reminder of the many ways that books connect us. "I'm sorry for your loss, though. That must be hard."

"We had a good life. A long time together. You can't ask for more. And that was Albert—always finding a way to keep me on my toes and sweep me off my feet." She fanned her face like she was fighting back tears. Her hair was styled in a short, spiky, modern cut. She wore it jet black with a touch of her natural gray weaved in, like a rock-star grandma.

"What's the name of your store?" I made myself comfortable, leaning back in my chair and folding my hands in my lap.

"The Last Chapter. Because this is my last and final chapter." Pink splotches spread across her cheeks. "I'm afraid you're going to think it's cheesy. My grandson teases me that it's too cliché. It is, I admit it, but I'm an old lady. I'm sentimental, and I'm fine with that. I remind him that aging is a gift. We're not promised tomorrow, so we might as well embrace today, cheesy or not."

"Not at all, I love it, and I completely agree," I said genuinely, taking an immediate liking to Laurel. She was spunky and unapologetically herself, two great traits in my opinion. "It's perfect, and you're right. You've earned your cheesiness. Where are you located?"

"Sacramento." She twisted the chain with her reading glasses dangling around her neck.

"Wonderful. That's close." I wanted to ask more, but the panel started. I took copious notes during the session and felt pleased that many of the suggestions the presenter offered were ways to build community—things like silent book clubs, bookstore date nights, and cook-from-the-book events where readers sampled delectable recipes from their favorite reads—that we were already doing at the Secret Bookcase.

"Oh dear, the list is never-ending, isn't it?" Laurel said when the panel wrapped. She dabbed her brow with the edge of her silky black scarf. "I may be too old for this. It's a lot to keep up with. I'm afraid I'm already getting left behind."

"You're never too old, and the truth is you can't do it all." I shook my head and met her eyes, hoping I could convince her not to get overwhelmed. Independent bookstores were the lifeblood of our communities. We needed more third spaces—safe places for readers to gather and connect, but creating that took time. "It's impossible," I said to her. "What I've learned over the years is to start with the low-hanging fruit, like a book club. Build that and then do the next thing and the next."

"You're too sweet. Thank you for the vote of confidence." She patted my arm. "You've convinced me. I'm saying it right now out loud—I am hosting my first book club when I return."

"See, you're already on your way." I smiled encouragingly.

"What session are you doing now?" She riffled through a pink canvas bag with the saying ONE MORE CHAPTER embroidered in a pale blue.

I checked the program. "I'm going to Fox's session."

"If you don't mind, I'll walk with you." She took her time getting up, moving slowly and deliberately like her joints hurt. She hooked one bag after the other on her shoulder, weighing down her left side. "I'm curious what he has to say about his technology. I don't trust him as far as I could throw him."

I doubted she could throw him far, but I didn't mention that as I waited for her to gather her things. "Do you know him?"

"Unfortunately, yes. He stopped by the store last month. You'd think I was being graced by the king with the way he behaved. He kept saying what an honor it was that he had chosen my store for a visit. He treated me like he expected me to bow down to him for merely coming into the Last Chapter. I'd never heard of him before that day."

"Was he visiting bookstores to promote his Headset?" The hallways and shared spaces were bustling in between sessions with the sound of happy chatter and bursts of color from the banners and book art. Heady scents of jasmine and sweet roses washed in from the pool deck.

We stopped to pick up boxed lunches and continued to the theater. Fox's session was sure to be popular, so I wasn't surprised it was being held in the largest venue. I waved to some familiar faces.

The bookselling world was small. Readers sometimes assumed that booksellers were competitive with each other, but the reality was that we tended to support each other. If we didn't carry a particular title, we would send customers to a nearby shop and vice versa. We often collaborated and brainstormed with our colleagues about ideas that were working in terms of front-of-store displays, events, and signings. I loved being a part of a community that cheered each other on.

"It's a long story." Laurel grabbed a lunch box and followed me into the theater. "Take it from me. He's not to be trusted. I plan on cornering him at some point this weekend and giving him a piece of my mind."

That sounded dramatic. Unfortunately, I didn't have a chance to ask her more because the panelists had taken their places. Next to Fox Andrews was Victor Moore, who created the Read Moore, an e-reader that automatically registers eye movements and suggests book selections. Phillip Kaufman, a longtime editor, was also joining the panel. According to the blurb in the program, he recently launched a new digital-first publishing house, Cloudbound. And Theodore Calodin, the owner of the Comic Vault, a graphic novel and manga shop, was moderating the panel.

"Uh—I—uh, want to say thanks for coming to our panel." Theodore held the microphone so close to his lips that it looked like he was about to swallow it. Despite his extreme proximity to the mic, his voice was barely audible.

"Louder," someone shouted. "We can't hear you."

Theodore spoke again at the same monotone volume, his speech halting with awkward pauses and stops and starts. He shifted uncomfortably, looking like he'd rather have a root canal than moderate the panel. "Um, yeah, so as a comic and game shop owner, um, my readers, uh, really enjoy living in their favorite fictional worlds for longer." He hesitated and then added, "That's why, uh, our DnD nights are popular." He stole a quick glance at his notes and turned to Fox, clearly eager to pass the mic. "Fox, can you tell us why you created the Headset?"

"Well, thanks for that rousing introduction." Fox stroked his goatee and rolled his eyes. Then he launched into a dissertation about world-building, gaming, and the future of reading from his lens, which was a fully immersive experience. "I know you ladies love Jane Austen. You aren't just going to read about the English countryside; you are going to be *in* the countryside with a shirtless Mr. Darcy. Are you feeling me?" He fanned his face as a handful of people let out an ooh. "That's right; it's getting hot in here, but not to be left out, where are my bros?"

A few hands raised, timidly.

"My dudes, do you love an epic space battle? Well, get ready because you're about to rocket into the next galaxy with the Headset." He droned on and on, not giving any time or space for his fellow panelists to speak. I didn't appreciate his assumption that only "his dudes" enjoyed an epic space battle or anything sci-fi. I wanted to raise my hand, rattle off some of my favorite sci-fi reads, and remind him that many of the greatest writers in the genre were women. Ursula Le Guin, Octavia Butler, Martha Wells, and Becky Chambers came to mind. Not to mention that plenty of men identified with Jane Austen. This past spring Liam and I had done a buddy read of *Emma*. He instantly fell in love with the historical details, Austen's unique ability to capture the constraints and culture of the time, and her incising, quick-witted humor. He'd gone on to read *Pride and Prejudice* and was moving on to *Sense and Sensibility* next, and we'd been working our way through the canon of Austen films. His personal favorite was the BBC's production with Colin Firth, but I had an equal soft spot for the Matthew Macfadyen adaptation. Honestly, was there ever a bad Darcy, though?

I opted to sit on my hands to keep from interrupting him to school him on his outdated and sexist perspective. Instead, I scanned the crowd, checking to see if anyone else was put off by his sentiment.

I spotted Serena Highbourn in the front row. She tapped her ear like a secret agent receiving covert instructions, then turned her attention to her tablet, her fingers flying wildly over the screen.

Was she transcribing the panel?

But why?

Maybe she was hoping to uncover some juicy book gossip at the convention?

It didn't seem like her usual subject matter, but maybe there was gossip brewing that I wasn't aware of.

"Uh, okay, if, um, Phillip—" Theodore tried to cut Fox off, but Fox just spoke over him.

When Fox finally paused long enough to catch a breath, Phillip jumped in. He was older and distinguished. He looked like he'd recently flown in from New York. California was casual. He was nothing but buttoned-up, from his crisp white shirt to his black suit jacket and matching skinny black tie. "If I may, I'd like to lend my perspective as someone who has worked for the Big Five, as we call them in the industry. This is potentially revolutionary for our writers as well. Suddenly, they won't be simply writing pages to be bound in a manuscript, but at my new publishing house, Cloudbound, we're exploring packages where new book deals would include the standard—print, e-book, and audio, and now VR as well."

"It's a disruptor," Victor cut him off. "We're changing the game, and you can be part of that." He thrust a finger at the audience.

"Victor, um, would you like to tell us more about, uh, how your Read Moore is also changing the industry?" Theodore asked quickly, trying to keep a grip on the conversation and give the other panelists any amount of airtime.

Victor was young. Really young. I'd guess him to be in his early twenties. He wore baggy cargo shorts and a Read Moore T-shirt. "I'd love to, since *some* of my fellow panelists have zero ethics and think they can swipe your ideas and get away with it." He wasn't subtle at throwing shade at Fox.

Fox pretended to be occupied with his Headset. He held it to the overhead stage lights, inspecting it with intense scrutiny.

"My proprietary technology will make your lives as booksellers much more efficient. You won't need to make recommendations. The Read Moore does it automatically. It registers the reader's interest based on eye movements and creates a curated reading list. You'll never again have to be bothered by customer requests for reading recommendations. My technology does it for you. Think of how much time it will save you."

"That's the best part of the job," a woman in front of us said out loud. "It's what we do."

I agreed. There was nothing better than matching a reader with their perfect book, and the reason I could do that was because I read nearly everything we had in the store. Hal,

Fletcher, and I had our areas of expertise, and we took it as a personal challenge to make sure every reader who left the store had a book that would keep them up late into the night, turning the pages.

"Eye movements?" Laurel caught my eye and made a face.

I opened my lunch box and unwrapped a turkey and Swiss sandwich with pesto and generous slices of heirloom tomatoes. I was going to need substance to get through this panel. The discussion became more heated and contentious. Victor and Fox were at odds on everything. If Victor said his market research showed readers preferred soft blue screens, Fox would counter that his research found the opposite.

Victor asked for a volunteer and brought up a bookseller from San Diego to showcase how the Read Moore worked.

Before Fox demoed the Headset, he played a video showing a few genre examples of the technology—a shot of dusty, red Mars from a sci-fi novel, Pemberley in the spring from Jane Austen, and a subway station in New York from a modern thriller.

It was hard to wrap my brain around the idea of virtual reality reading. For me, reading meant curling up in a quiet corner with a cup of tea and Professor Plum, my cat, on my lap. I loved that, depending on a book's pacing, I might take a leisurely stroll through the Cotswolds, conjuring up my own images of the characters and village. Fox's Headset did that for me. There was no need to create a vision to pair with the story or try to slip into the author's head. The Headset put me into the story for sure, but I wasn't positive that's what I wanted.

"Now I'll give you a real-time demonstration. I'll read a passage out loud, and you'll see what I see in the Headset on the screen behind me. Prepare to have your mind blown." Fox cued the lighting tech and Theodore. The lights dimmed as he placed the Headset over his ears. He reached for his phone and twisted the dial on the side of the Headset.

I expected him to begin reading, but the lights flickered, and a high-pitched, piercing sound reverberated through the room. I stuffed my fingers in my ears. It was like a bad feedback loop.

Fox fiddled with the settings.

As he turned the dial again, his eyes grew wide.

Then there was a terrible popping—an explosion. The power went out, but not before I noticed Fox's head slump and fall lifeless to the table.

FIVE

"He's dead! Fox is dead!" Victor screamed and jumped away from the table like it was on fire.

"Oh dear. I think I might faint." Laurel reached for me with a quivering hand. Her body swayed in her seat like she was about to pass out.

At least she was sitting. "Keep breathing. Stay here. I need to help," I said, clutching her wrist and making solid eye contact. "It's going to be okay."

She managed to nod but couldn't tear her eyes away from the stage. The theater went ghostly quiet. Everyone sat in stunned silence.

Victor, Theodore, and Phillip were all on their feet and moving toward Fox's lifeless body.

"Don't touch him," I cautioned, sprinting down the aisle.

The lights flickered on again with a hum. I wondered if the generator had kicked in. I raced to the stage and motioned for them to back away from the table and Fox's body.

"Uh, what happened? Maybe, um, a short circuit?" Theodore shielded his face with his hand, trying to avoid catching a glimpse of Fox.

I didn't blame him, but I also needed to take charge and control the scene until the police arrived. Fox's death might be an unfortunate accident, or it might be murder. I couldn't risk anyone contaminating the crime scene. "Call 911," I said to Theodore. "You should both sit down," I directed Victor and Phillip. Then I took the stage and addressed the crowd. "I'm Annie Murray. I'm a bookseller and a private investigator, and the best thing we can do is remain calm. I encourage you to remain in your seats. This is a terrible tragedy. The authorities are on their way and will advise us of the next steps, but until they arrive, it's critical we all stay calm and stay put."

The audience murmured in agreement.

I approached Fox's body. He had the telltale signs of electrocution. His wiry hair stood at attention like he'd been zapped by lightning. His face was ruby red. I suspected his eyes were frozen wide open in fear, but they were hidden by the VR headset.

"What happened?" Phillip asked, grabbing his suit jacket from the back of his chair. He smoothed an errant strand of his dark hair by licking his finger and massaging his head.

"It's too soon to say," I lied. I didn't want to plant any ideas in his mind until the police had an opportunity to take his statement, but I had a bad feeling about this.

Why had Fox inspected the Headset so closely right before he died?

And a Headset shouldn't blow up. That couldn't be normal. Something wasn't right. My mind raced to make connections and replay every detail leading up to the moment Fox placed the Headset on his head.

"He pressed that button on the side of the Headset, and it was like it exploded or something," Victor said, leaning closer to the table to inspect the technology. "It happened so fast. It had to be the Headset, right? I warned him that he was rushing it to market too fast. He wouldn't listen."

"Rushing it?" I asked. Could the technology be faulty? If Fox had hurried the process to get the Headset ready for the trade show, that could explain the mishap and potentially mean his death was indeed an accident.

Victor nodded, rubbing his temples like he was trying to release pent-up tension. "He was crazed. He was like a mad scientist, desperate to launch his Frankenstein into the world."

Technically, it was Frankenstein's monster if we were speaking in literary terms, but I wasn't surprised he got the reference wrong. He had clearly skimmed bookish references at best. I considered calling him out, but I doubted he would care.

"Frankenstein? Jealous much, my friend?" Phillip interjected, loosening his tie, like he was trying to get more air.

"It is a Frankenstein. Look at him." Victor threw his hands up. "I warned him he wasn't ready. You can't rush tech like this. It has to go through the proper protocols and testing. Imagine if he'd demoed the Headset on a bookseller. A lawsuit like that would bankrupt him immediately."

"Right, but he's dead," Phillip said, shaking his head in disgust. "I'm not buying your forced empathy. I heard you two arguing before the panel. I know you were trying to stop the Headset's release, so don't play games with me. I heard every word you said." He paused for effect. "Every word."

A cold chill spread through my veins. Everything about the scene felt wrong. I took mental notes. I had no idea yet how this information might play into the investigation, but any insight into Fox Andrews and his virtual reality product could prove beneficial later.

Victor clenched his fists. His posture became rigid as his nostrils flared. It looked like he was barely containing an outburst. I half expected him to lunge at Phillip, and I didn't have time to deal with a fight. We had a dead body to deal with first.

Theodore finished the call. His hands quaked as he tried

to stuff his phone into his cargo shorts. "Uh, they'll be here any minute." He tugged his graphic T-shirt away from his body and scanned the theater like he was searching for an exit.

"Good." I wondered how quickly word would spread once the hotel was teeming with uniformed police officers and first responders. "None of you used the Headset? Did anyone touch it before Fox put it on?"

They shook their heads. "Fox wouldn't let us near his 'baby,' as he referred to the Headset," Victor answered with a snarl curling on his lips. "He was convinced that another company would copy his technology and release it first. His lab was locked down. He was super paranoid about corporate espionage. It was like Area 51. No one got in or out." Beads of sweat pooled on Victor's forehead. He used his Read Moore T-shirt sleeve to mop his brow.

"Do you think there was any truth to the idea there might be corporate espionage?" I asked, studying the table. My mind raced to make furious calculations. Other than their notes and water bottles, there wasn't anything out of place. Each seat had its own microphone. I glanced at the wiring—could it have accidentally sparked?

Victor scoffed, pulling my attention back. "Please. No. What a joke. Fox had an inflated ego. It's not like VR is a new concept. He wasn't reinventing the wheel. He was taking tech that already exists and putting a book spin on it."

I got the sense that someone was tuned in to our conversation. I could feel eyes on me. As I turned in that direction, sure enough, Serena Highbourn was ignoring my orders and approaching the front of the stage.

She yanked her earbuds out and tapped an expensive diamond-encrusted silver watch. "I can't stay. I'm due for a signing in the book hall. You'll have to let the authorities know they can speak with me later. They'll be able to find me. Just look for the crowd of fans. I'm sure the line is already halfway out the door."

"I'm sorry, I can't let you leave," I said, planting my feet firmly on the stage. "The police will be here any minute."

I was about to say more about protocol in situations like this, but she cut me off.

"Do you know who I am? I am Serena Highbourn." She stuffed her earbuds into her purse and tossed her long white hair over one shoulder. "I'm not a no-name indie author off the street. The organizers flew me in from London last night. My readers are surely already queued up, waiting for me. I refuse to leave them in the lurch. It's extremely unprofessional."

"These are not normal circumstances," I said with authority, checking the doorway, hoping the police would show up. I wasn't sure how long I would be able to keep Serena in the auditorium; if she left, it would likely start a mass exodus.

"I'd listen to Annie," Phillip said, backing me up. "You're going to want to get out in front of this, given your history with Fox."

Serena flinched. "What is that supposed to mean? You're one to talk, Phillip."

They exchanged a look I couldn't quite decipher, but the tension between them was palpable.

Just then, the police and paramedics arrived and immediately took over. A frenzy of activity changed the energy in the theater. Suddenly, people started to chatter as the team of uniformed officers swept through the crowd and barked out orders.

I watched as the paramedics assessed Fox for any life signs, and officers began constructing a barrier around the table.

"You secured the scene?" a woman asked me. She was young—probably about my age with dark eyes and a heart-shaped face. She wore a creamy silk tank layered with a lightweight blazer and slim-fitting charcoal slacks. Her hair was tied in a high ponytail. She appraised me carefully, yet warmly, reminding me of a younger Dr. Caldwell.

"Yes, I'm Annie Murray. I'm here for the conference as a bookseller, but I'm also a private detective and have a degree in criminology." I gave her a very brief history, mentioning Dr. Caldwell. I doubted she would be familiar with my mentor, but it never hurt to name-drop. "I might be jumping to conclusions, but something about this doesn't sit right." I relayed everything I'd seen leading up to the moment Fox put the Headset on in exacting detail. The first moments after a crime were critical, and I didn't want to forget a single thing. The slightest detail that might seem insignificant could later break a case open— something as simple as Fox inspecting the Headset right before his death.

She listened with interest, tipping her head to one side when I finished and letting out a little laugh that made her ponytail swing from side to side. "Okay. You weren't kidding. You are professionally trained, aren't you? That was a very detailed assessment. Thank you."

"I'm officially licensed as a private investigator now, and I don't know about you, but I've learned to trust my gut. My gut is screaming that this wasn't an accident." I showed her my credentials.

"Yeah, I agree. Excellent. Well done. Thank you for helping," she said, twisting a strand of hair that had fallen from her ponytail. "I'm Detective Greene. If you don't mind waiting while we assess the victim and gather intel, I will likely have some additional questions for you."

"Of course." I hung to the side of the stage while the paramedics carefully removed the Headset. The police squad took photos while the officer I had spoken with addressed the audience. As I expected, she explained that they would need everyone's contact information and statements before she could release the room.

Serena tried to plead her case, but Detective Greene didn't budge. "I'm sorry. There are no exceptions, ma'am. This is a crime scene."

The bestselling author slunk into her seat in the front row and sighed audibly. She tucked her earbuds in and began taking rapid notes on her tablet. I wondered if Fox's death was going to work its way into her next book.

While I waited to be interviewed, I texted Dr. Caldwell.

> There's been a death at the conference.

I gave her a quick overview of what had happened.

> I'm sure you'll be of great assistance. Text or call if I can help in any way. Does this derail your mission?

I assured her that Fox's death wouldn't interfere with my plans, and then I looped Hal in, too. I knew he'd be hurt if he found out from someone else. Given how quickly news spread on social media and how many fellow booksellers were in attendance, that wasn't out of the question.

> Don't freak out, but there's been an accident.

> I hope this doesn't portend to other things. Please be safe, Annie. And tell Fletcher I say the same to him.

He didn't need to elaborate. I understood the context.

I felt better knowing they were both aware of the incident. I considered checking in with Liam, too. It was funny to think about how much a part of my life he'd become. He was the first person I wanted to tell anything—good or bad. But I knew he would only worry, so I decided against it. We could hash everything out once he and Pri arrived. Just knowing they were on their way made me feel instantly better.

I was impressed by the swift police response. Detective Greene worked efficiently and effectively. She spent extra time with Fox's fellow panelists—Victor, Phillip, and Theodore. I didn't want to leap to conclusions, but her response and the paramedics made me fairly certain they suspected foul play.

What were the odds that a VR headset would electrocute Fox?

I was relatively tech-savvy, and I couldn't figure out how the Headset had enough power to deliver a fatal shock. Could someone have tampered with it? Perhaps the killer rewired it to trigger a powerful electric shock. I had more questions than answers at this point, but all signs pointed to Fox being murdered.

SIX

Detective Greene called me over to the center of the stage. "Ms. Murray, I'm ready for you now."

The table and microphones had been roped off with police caution tape. Her team noted evidence with small yellow markers and dusted for fingerprints. The auditorium had emptied now, giving it a cold, eerie vibe. The reality that Fox had died right in front of hundreds of people was starting to sink in.

Officers flanked each exit door, directing people and ensuring no one entered.

"Sorry to keep you." Detective Greene unzipped her sleek crossbody bag and removed a small sage-green soft leather notebook. We sold the brand at the Secret Bookcase. It was popular with writers and sketch artists and now, apparently, police officers. "Your initial assessment of the scene gives me a lot to work with—super thorough. Thank you. I'll be honest; this is only my third solo case, so I could use any help I can get. And I'm with you; something about this feels wrong. You mentioned a gut instinct—I have one, too."

"I'm happy to help however I can, and yeah, my criminology professor used to tell us always to trust our gut."

"Yeah, I agree. Sometimes you just can't shake that sixth sense that something is off." She pursed her lips into a tight smile and nodded like she had already made her mind up that she wanted to work with me. "I'm glad you're game to help, because having a private detective on the inside for the next couple of days certainly gives me a leg up. Also, I have to confess, when I checked your credentials, I took a quick look at the Secret Bookcase's social media accounts, and oh my God, what a dream. I'm a huge mystery fan. I read my grandma's Nancy Drew books growing up. That's what made me want to become a detective. How did I never know about your store?"

I smiled. "We're a little off the beaten path, but it's totally worth a day trip, especially if you're a mystery lover." I felt an instant kinship to her, and in that moment a memory of Scarlet resurfaced.

I wandered into the HUB, the student center on campus for trivia night, scanning the crowded room for any familiar faces. It was only my third week of classes, and since I've always tended to be a bit of an introvert, at least until I got to know someone, there were none. Well, technically, there was a guy from my Bio 101. But he had argued for a good twenty minutes with our professor about how chemtrails weren't merely water vapor, but rather an elaborate secret government plan to release mind-control chemicals, so he was an immediate pass in my book.

I almost considered leaving and sneaking back to my dorm room where I had a stack of fresh new library books and a care package from my parents waiting.

No, Annie, you can do this. You need to do this.

I refused to let my bookish tendencies taint my collegiate experience. I needed to put myself out there and make friends.

Trivia night was a first step, so I approached a table with three women my age.

"Is this seat open?" I asked one of them, deciding at that moment that if she said no, it would be a sign from the universe that I could retreat to the safety of my room.

She was tall with olive skin and silky dark hair. Her eyelids were dusted with purple shadow and her expression held a subtle cleverness, as if she had already unraveled everyone's secrets but would never tell. "It's all yours. Join us." She tapped the back of a chair.

I slipped into the seat, timidly.

"This is our first trivia night, so fair warning, we might be terrible," she said with a self-deprecating grin. "The most important thing to know is it's *Jeopardy*-style, so be sure to answer the question with the question."

"Got it," I replied, feeling the tension in my body ease a little. "I'm terrible, too. Unless it's books. If it's a book question, I should be pretty good."

"All right, girls, we've got books covered," she announced to the rest of the table.

The trivia host cut any further introductions short as they launched into the first question. "This iconic mystery board game was first released in 1949, and challenges players to deduce who, where, and how a murder has occurred with characters like Colonel Mustard and Miss Scarlet."

In unison, the two of us shouted, "What is Clue?"

She turned to high-five me, grinning. "Well, I guess we're going to be best friends. I'm Scarlet. Miss Scarlet, if you will."

I smiled internally at the memory of our instant bond. From that moment on, Scarlet and I were inseparable. But that was also long, long ago, and now I had a chance to deliver justice for her finally.

Detective Greene flipped through the notebook to a blank page, pulling me fully into the present.

I wondered if she felt the same about me, given our age and gender. The field of police and detective work was slowly changing, emphasis on *slowly*. But men still vastly outnumbered women. The gender imbalance in the profession was glaringly obvious. Dr. Caldwell recently shared statistics from the previous year. Women accounted for less than 18 percent of full-time law enforcement officers and less than 17 percent of detectives.

"Can you walk me through what you witnessed one more time?" she asked, readjusting the leather badge holder clipped to her pants.

I shifted into investigative mode. Scarlet had led me here. She'd been with me like a silent partner for all these years, pushing me forward, reminding me I was meant to do this kind of work. "The panel started without any issues, although there was clear animosity between Fox and the other speakers."

"Tell me more about that," she encouraged.

I shared my observations and the snippets of conversation I'd heard.

"That checks with other eyewitness statements." She made a few notes, considering everything I'd told her. "Think back again, when the incident occurred, did you notice anything unusual?"

I closed my eyes and replayed the scene. "Yes. It was subtle, but I got the sense that Fox was frustrated with the Headset. When Victor finally had a chance to speak, Fox became preoccupied with the Headset. At first, I assumed he was disinterested in hearing what any of the other panelists had to say, but then I realized he was inspecting the device. He kept tapping the buttons on the side like it wasn't working as he intended. Then the last tap was the fatal blow." I shuddered at the memory of seeing his body jolt and then slump over in his chair.

"I'm sending the Headset to our tech department for analysis," she said without hesitation.

"Do you think someone tampered with it?"

She paused and glanced around to make sure there was no one in earshot, except for her crew of officers who were continuing the painstaking process of securing the scene and ensuring every last shred of evidence was collected. "That's my working theory. Virtual headsets don't just implode, do they?" She tapped her finger to her temple as if signaling she'd already thought this through.

"Right." I nodded. "That's what I keep coming back to as well." Part of me felt validated that I had reached the same conclusion, but that meant Fox's murder had been premeditated, and a killer was among us.

She leaned back slightly, with her arms crossed, as if daring anyone to argue with her. "Listen, I'd love you to help on this. I can't extend you an official consulting contract without approval, which could take a while, but I'll submit the paperwork when I return to the office. That is, if you're interested?" She looked at me expectantly.

"Yes, of course." I was flattered she wanted my help and not-so-secretly happy to have a reason to look into Fox's death. "My colleague Fletcher is here at the conference with me; we're setting up our agency together and I know he'll be glad to help, too."

"Good. In the meantime, if you're willing to be another set of eyes and ears for us, I'd appreciate any insight you might be able to offer. You're a professional, so you understand the bounds of how you operate with your private license."

I knew exactly what she was hinting at. As a private investigator, I had no legal authority in the case. However, I could work discreetly to gather evidence and speak with individuals who may be more reluctant to share with the police.

"I'd like you to act as a liaison and bridge whatever trust

gaps you can," she continued, readjusting her ponytail. "You've already interacted with a number of the witnesses and potential suspects. Any insight into their motives, relationships, and history would be much appreciated and very useful."

"Absolutely." I took my role seriously. One of the many things I'd studied in preparation for my exam was the importance of collaboration with law enforcement. Dr. Caldwell had already extended offers for Fletcher and me to consult whenever the opportunity arose, and this was an opportunity to expand our reach.

"Excellent." She reached into her thin suit jacket and handed me a business card. "I'll be in and out, but please text or call if you learn anything you think might be pertinent. I'll check in later, although seriously, I wish I could hang out—this is so cool. A book convention. I'm envious."

I left her in the auditorium as the paramedics began loading Fox's body onto a stretcher. This was a turn of events I had never anticipated. I'd been so focused on Silicon Summit Partners and my plan to infiltrate the brokerage firm. Not in my wildest imagination would I have thought a murder would occur at a booksellers' convention.

The lobby and common areas were buzzing. Everyone was rattled and talking about Fox's murder. I scanned the crowd, searching for Fletcher. He was at the coffee station fueling up.

"Hey, you've heard the news, right?" I scooted into line behind him.

"Uh, yeah. I've been desperate to find you. I can't believe I skipped that panel. Did Fox die right in front of you? I should have come with you." He shook his head in stunned disbelief.

"No, trust me, you don't want that image in your head." I closed my eyes and tried to mentally erase the picture of Fox placing the Headset over his eyes.

He poured cream into his coffee and stirred it with a

wooden stick. "I'm so insensitive sometimes, sorry. I didn't mean it like that."

"I know you didn't." I poured half decaf and half regular into a paper mug and helped myself to a cinnamon raisin oatmeal cookie.

"Should we sit?" Fletcher motioned to the veranda doors. "I see an open spot outside."

"Yeah, that would be great." I could use a minute to collect my thoughts and review everything that had happened with Fletcher while it was still fresh.

The afternoon sun felt good on my skin. We found seats near the pool with a bright yellow sun umbrella that provided just the right amount of shade. Large potted succulents added a pop of greenery to the deck. Two young kids practiced their cannonball technique at the opposite end of the pool, challenging each other to see who could make the biggest splash.

I smiled. The fact that life proceeded on in the midst of death always brought me an equal sense of reassurance and sadness. Fox was only in his thirties. His career was just beginning. Regardless of his ego or his business practices, he didn't deserve to die.

"Tell me everything." Fletcher leaned back against the chair and loosened his scarf, letting it fall around his long, narrow neck.

How he wasn't drenched in sweat was a mystery to me. It had to be nearly eighty degrees out here, but he remained committed to his fashion statement. I could feel the warmth on my skin and guessed that my freckles were likely turning a bright shade of cinnamon in the heat.

"Where to start?" I broke off a chunk of the cookie. It was sweet and spicy with a pop of tang from the raisins.

"The beginning?" He raised an eyebrow and rested his chin on his hands like he was preparing to listen.

That was one of the many things I appreciated about our

friendship. Fletcher had plenty of quirks and tended to drone on for hours about irrelevant, obscure Sherlockian facts, but he was a good listener, an active listener who asked leading questions while at the same time making space for me to say whatever I needed to. Our conversations tended to lead to revelations both from his thoughtful questions and his insight.

I polished off the cookie and launched into my story, not sparing any of the gory details.

Fletcher sipped his coffee and listened intently, stopping me several times for clarification. "Detective Greene wants us to assist in the investigation?"

"Yes. She's great. She loves mysteries. I told her she needs to come visit the Secret Bookcase." My eyes drifted to the poolside bar with its polished wood counter and vintage signage. It was opening for lunch service, and people were already queuing for colorful cocktails served in frosted glasses with paper drink umbrellas. The scent of grilling pineapple and sausages wafted toward us, making my stomach rumble even though I wasn't hungry. "She was clear that we have to follow procedure and protocol."

"As we would," he interrupted, like he was put out that she would suggest otherwise. "Although I like her already. Clearly, she has excellent reading taste."

"True, and she's aware of my background and the Novel Detectives," I said, dragging my eyes away from the bar. "That goes without saying."

"Good, because we are consummate professionals; I hope she understands that." Fletcher sounded half-serious, half-sarcastic. His dry sense of humor came through. I appreciated that he was never above a touch of self-deprecation.

I smiled softly. "I don't think she'd loop us in on the case if she didn't."

"Touché." He raised his cup. "It sounds like Fox had plenty of people who were less than thrilled with his invention."

"Yeah, that's an understatement. No one on the panel seemed excited to be sharing the stage with him, to say the very least. Victor is at the top of my list. He flat-out accused Fox of stealing technology."

"That gives him a strong motive." Fletcher swirled his coffee cup like he was drinking fine wine. "What about the other two?"

"Theodore is your typical comic-shop geek. I got the impression he was intimidated by Fox, but I need to speak with him one-on-one and see if he'll open up more. Fox steamrolled him during the panel. He was super nervous. That could be because he was out of his league and uncomfortable with public speaking, but he was sweating profusely—like a leaky water faucet— and clearly jittery and on edge."

"I can't blame him on the public speaking," Fletcher said with a shudder. "Fox cutting him off is annoying but hardly a reason to kill him."

"Right. We need to learn as much as possible about Fox's prior connection to each of them. Phillip, too. He mentioned that his new publishing firm is stepping into the VR space as well."

"Do you think they were partners? Maybe a business relationship that went south?" Fletcher suggested.

"Possibly. It's something we should explore. Serena High-bourn was furious with Fox. They argued, and even the woman sitting next to me, Laurel Deters, who owns a new bookstore, the Last Chapter, mentioned that he came by her shop. She wasn't a fan, but we never had a chance to go into detail. I want to make sure I follow up with her, too."

"It sounds like we have our work cut out for us." Fletcher glanced around the shimmery pool.

The cannonballers had discovered the diving board and were trying to outdo each other to see who could catch the most air. Small groups had broken off and taken over the cabanas and poolside seating. I wondered if the afternoon sessions would continue or if Fox's murder would put a pause on the convention. I kicked myself for not asking Detective Greene about that.

"Have you heard whether the next round of panels is happening?" I brushed cookie crumbs from my dress. I was torn because I could already feel the pull toward wanting to piece together what happened to Fox, but Scarlet remained top of my mind. I couldn't lose sight of why I was here.

He reached for his schedule and nodded. "According to the organizers, they're taking a short break, and everything will continue except for anything scheduled to be in the auditorium. I believe they're finding a new space for those panels and talks."

"Okay. Should we divide and conquer? I'll start with Theodore and Laurel. Why don't you do some digging into Victor Moore? I'd like to know as much as possible about his product, the Read Moore."

"You're speaking my language, Annie. Should we plan to reconvene for happy hour?"

"Yes." I stood and glanced around us, leaning closer to him and lowering my voice. "Fletcher, be careful. If Fox was murdered, his killer put plenty of time, thought, and energy into plotting his death. We don't know who we're dealing with."

"I'll use the utmost caution." Fletcher wrapped his scarf tighter, gathered our empty coffee cups, and strolled inside.

I had to remember my own advice. Fox's murder wasn't a spur-of-the-moment crime of passion. Whoever killed him went to great lengths to re-wire his Headset and ensure that Fox wore it for the demonstration. If they realized Fletcher and I were part of the investigation, we could be next.

SEVEN

Laurel found me first. "Oh, there you are. I've been looking everywhere for you." She fiddled with her book totes, taking them on and off her shoulder like she couldn't get comfortable. "You won't believe the questions the police asked me. It's as if they think I had something to do with Fox's accident. Me? A grandmother. Can you believe that?"

I'd listened to Detective Greene's questions. She had done everything by the book. Her questions were standard, and it was normal protocol to take statements from witnesses in a case like this. Laurel shouldn't have anything to worry about. "How so?" I asked Laurel.

She yanked one of the bags off her shoulder one last time and looped it around her wrist. "It was a litany of questions—starting with if I'd met him before. I should have lied, but as soon as the police learned that he had visited my store, they treated me like a common criminal."

That seemed like an overstatement. Detective Greene's style was anything but harsh or overbearing.

"You mentioned he came by your store. What happened?" I

hoped this was my way to hear more about her relationship with Fox Andrews.

"Where do I even start?" She sighed and ran her hands through her spiky hair, making it stick out in every direction. "He stopped in to grace me with his presence a few weeks after I opened. He took dozens and dozens of videos and photos of the store. I thought it was odd at the time, but frankly, I was thrilled to have anyone browsing. Buying would be better, but just getting bodies into the store has been more challenging than I realized. I found a cute retail spot in a nice little up-and-coming neighborhood of Sacramento, but the problem is we don't get much foot traffic." She paused to catch her breath.

I was about to tell her that foot traffic was a common issue, but she continued before I could get a word in.

"I've done everything I can think of to attract new readers into the Last Chapter, but nothing seems to be working. I've been running ads, and my grandson has helped me with my website and social media. He's quite the technology wiz. I've offered specials and discounts, but none of my marketing is pulling in enough customers to keep the lights on. I'm worried that if sales continue remaining slow, I'll have to close within the year. Poor Albert. He saved a nest egg for my dream, and I'm going to run it into the ground. This isn't what I imagined owning a bookstore would be like." She twirled the bag straps around her arm. "I should know better. I'm in my seventies; you'd think I'd have some life experience by now, but I honestly believed I'd be spending my days leafing through my favorite reads and chatting with customers."

"Isn't that the dream?" I chuckled. I wanted to validate her struggles and also find a way to get back on track regarding Fox. "There's a pervasive myth that running a bookshop is unicorns and roses, reading all day, and flying famous authors in for packed book signings, but the truth is that retail is a hard and long game. Building a loyal customer base takes time, and it always requires staying nimble. Sure, there are slow moments when I can flip through the pages of a book, but there's so much back-end work customers don't see—inventory, restocking the shelves, returns, curating displays, book research, event planning, cleaning, organizing, the list goes on and on. That's why coming to a convention like this will probably be a great boost for your morale. You're not alone. Every bookseller faces the same challenges. Don't give up yet. It's too soon."

She blinked back tears. "Thank you, dear. I'm sorry to unload on you. I realize I can talk too much. It's been a stressful time, and then seeing Fox..." She trailed off.

"I know. It's okay. It was terrible." I wished the memory and the sound hadn't been imprinted on my brain. "So he came into your store to take pictures and video? Was there a reason?"

Laurel's body shifted. Her jaw tightened, and her eyes narrowed into tiny slits. "Oh yes, there was a reason. He used the footage he took in the Last Chapter. *My* bookstore is now the Headset's virtual reality cozy bookstore. It's a travesty."

"What?" I tried to keep my tone neutral, but this was a big revelation and potentially gave Laurel a motive for killing him.

Her thin lips pressed together firmly into a hard, unbroken line, erasing any hint of softness in her expression. "It makes my blood boil every time I think about it. He didn't disclose what he was doing. I suppose, technically, he asked if it was okay to take photos and videos, but I thought that was because he was impressed with my shop. Flattery will get you everywhere, won't it? He kept saying things like, 'This is so charming and quaint.' I'm an idiot for trusting him. I should have realized he was up to no good."

"He used the images for his Headset?" I was curious how that could be legal.

"Yes. He was going to debut his virtual reality bookstore at the panel. I got a first look from his marketing team." She fidgeted with her tote bags, pushing them up over her shoulder and clutching the handles tightly like she was trying to regain control of her emotions. "The audacity. They tried to spin it like I should be grateful to him. He stole my shop. There's no mention of the Last Chapter in his demo. He used my store as his baseline for his designs and then digitally enhanced it. Those are his words, not mine, by the way. That was his legal loophole. He took a video of me saying it was fine to film in the store and used that as my approval. I never would have approved if I knew what he intended to do with the images."

"Did you seek legal help?" None of this sounded aboveboard.

"I don't have extra cash lying around." She laced her fingers together, shielding her body with the totes. "I did ask a friend who is a lawyer, and they said because I'm on film agreeing that it's okay for him to shoot, it would be a hard case to prove. I still can't believe I was so naïve. Now I have signs posted everywhere in the store saying: No Photos or Filming. I hate that I had to do that. I want to trust my customers, but Fox ruined that."

"So he created a virtual reality bookstore as part of the Headset?" I wanted to make sure I was getting a clear picture of what had transpired between them so that I could report it to Detective Greene.

"Not just any store—a shoppable store. He was going to profit off my blood, sweat, and tears. While in his virtual store, readers can simply point to what they want, and it appears in their shopping cart." Her tone turned sharp like the prickly tip of a pencil. "He was bragging about how easy it would be to build a never-ending reading list with the Headset. Translation —put small mom-and-pop shops like me out of business while using the charm of my store to sell more digital books."

I was glad Laurel had opened up to me. This information directly related to his death and, unfortunately, gave her a clear motive for killing him. The only problem was that she didn't strike me as technically savvy. Could she have figured out how to jerry-rig the Headset? Or maybe her grandson helped her with that, too.

"It's terrible to speak ill of the dead, but I admit I'm not heartbroken about his accident." She cleared her throat. "I'm sorry to say that. It's out of character for me. My Albert used to tease that I was too tender-hearted. I always try to rescue everyone I meet. Our Thanksgiving table every year is filled with strangers I meet at the grocery store or friends of friends with no place to go. He left a note in his will to remind me not to give away all the books once I opened the shop and try to make at least enough to get by. He knew me too well. I don't care about getting rich. Owning the Last Chapter is my lifelong dream. But Fox was a conniving liar and a cheat. I don't have much sympathy for him." She caught herself. "Don't get me wrong, it's terrible he's dead, but you're not going to see me shedding a tear for that vile man."

Her personality had shifted. Gone was the sweet, elderly bookstore owner living out her dream. In her place was a hardened woman with an axe to grind. Not that I entirely blamed her. If Fox had visited the Secret Bookcase under the guise of being a casual shopper, and then we discovered he'd been shooting footage to build his digital virtual reality store, I would be furious, too.

The question was, could she have been furious enough to kill him? And how had she managed it?

"You must think I'm horrid." Laurel pressed her hand to her head like she was checking her temperature.

"I'm sure it's complicated," I said, although I was beginning to reconsider my first impression of her.

A ding echoed in the lobby, followed by an announcement informing us the next round of panels was starting soon.

"Is it time already?" She gathered her book bags and leafed through the program. "I'm attending the session on social media marketing. Lord knows I need all the help I can get in that department. Will I see you there or later at the happy hour reception?"

"Happy hour, for sure. I haven't decided what I'm going to do yet." That was half-true. I planned to track down Theodore next.

"Excellent. I'll find you later. And please accept my apologies for talking your ear off. It's been good to get this off my chest, but I fear I've unloaded my problems onto you, which was not my intention."

"Don't give it a thought." I waved her off. "Enjoy the social media panel. I'll be eager to hear what you learn later."

"You're an angel, thanks for listening." Laurel blew me a kiss and skirted past a group of book cosplay readers dressed like their favorite manga characters.

I watched her disappear into the crowd and absently adjusted my glasses even though they were already securely in place. It was a habitual movement Liam never failed to tease me about. He'd smirk and say, "I can always tell when you're thinking, Murray—your glasses haven't even slipped, but you're fixing them anyway." I smiled at the thought and let my focus drift to the ceiling, staring at the white popcorn-like texture as if the answers to my many questions were floating above me. Laurel didn't exactly fit the profile of a killer, but she had a strong, emotional motive for murdering Fox. I wasn't ready to rule her out yet, and I had plenty of new information to share with Detective Greene.

EIGHT

I followed the manga group, figuring I might find Theodore wherever they ended up. My hunch was correct. They led me to a small conference room at the very back of the hotel, where two comic book artists were signing copies of their latest releases.

It was hard not to get caught up in oohing and aahing over the elaborate and colorful costumes. Readers had gone all out for the event with kimonos, plastic swords, knee-high tights, capes, wigs, and makeup. I snapped a bunch of photos and selfies to share with our followers on social media, posing with Dorothy from *The Wizard of Oz* with a Barbie house smashed on her shoulders and a Where's Waldo with a stocking cap, red-and-white-striped shirt, blue pants, and a wooden cane.

The conference room was decked out with gaming posters and a variety of pop culture merchandise, from bobbleheads to miniature figurines, board games, and cards.

I spotted Theodore standing near the signing table, handing out sticky notes for readers to write their names on in order to get their comics appropriately signed.

I hovered near the table, waiting for a lull in the line to

speak with him. As soon as a moment presented itself, I approached him with a nod. "How's it going?"

Theodore looked at me with surprise, like it was taking him a minute to place how he knew me. He squinted and scrunched his nose as he jutted his chin forward to get a better look at me.

"It's Annie Murray." I pointed to the badge hanging around my neck. "I was at the panel with Fox." I extended my hand. How had he already forgotten me?

"Okay, uh, yeah, gotcha. Yeah, um, sorry. I'm, uh, not good with faces. Or names, actually. After what happened with Fox, I think, uh, I sort of blacked out for a minute there." He wiped his hands on his pants and gave me a clammy shake. His face was blotched with red marks and damp sweat. "I get nervous meeting new people, and I'm still freaked out by what happened. I can't believe he's—he's... dead."

I wondered how that played out with owning a small store. Theodore must be meeting new people every day, in theory.

"We're all in shock." I nodded, hoping to put him at ease. It was clear that Theodore was an introvert. If I had any chance of getting through to him, I needed to meet him where he was at.

"It's so shocking, like, uh, literally shocking. How did it happen?" He rubbed his legs vigorously as if trying to get blood flowing. It was obviously a rhetorical question because he kept going. "I can't stop thinking about him and seeing him." He winced and shut his eyes tight.

A reader dressed like Hello Kitty approached for a sticky note.

Theodore handed one to her and set the stack on the edge of the table. He pointed to the corner of the room. "I don't want to talk about this here with so many people around, but I do have a question for you."

"Sure." I followed him.

He leaned against the wall, only to snag his back on a poster advertising a new video game. "Oh, uh, shoot," he muttered, quickly smoothing and straightening the poster, keeping his hand on it for a minute to make sure it stayed in place. "The police are everywhere. The detective was watching me. Did you see her when you came in?"

I glanced around the room. There was no sign of Detective Greene or any of her team. "No, why?"

"She's watching me," he repeated, his eyes darting from one side of the room to the other. "Maybe it's, uh, because I've read too many comics and superhero stories, but it's always the nerdy, quiet guy. She thinks I did it. I can just tell."

"I doubt that. It's her job to interview every witness. You were on the panel with Fox, and you were right there when it happened. I'm sure it's standard procedure." What I didn't say to him was that his skittish behavior was likely a red flag for Detective Greene.

"I guess you could be right, but she's tough. She was grilling me for a half hour. I don't do well in the heat." He glanced at his shirt, which was splotched with sweat stains. "I, uh, get over-heated pretty easily. She kept asking technical questions about the Headset. Just because I own a comic shop doesn't mean I'm a tech wizard."

As if on cue, a young reader dressed like a wizard with a shiny purple cape and pointy hat passed by us.

"She was asking you about the Headset technology?" Again, I wasn't sure I agreed with his assessment of Detective Greene. Both he and Laurel seemed to interpret her questioning as some sort of a personal attack.

"Yep. Just because Fox was going to debut at the Comic Vault, my store, she assumed I understood how it operates." He yanked a tack from the poster and rubbed it between his fingers.

"Fox was planning to showcase the Headset at your store?" I could hear the surprise in my tone.

Theodore sucked in a breath and leaned further into the wall like he was trying to disappear. "It's a long story."

"If you're willing to share, I'd love to hear your perspective on Fox. I was chatting with another bookstore owner who had a bad experience with him." I hoped that sharing Laurel's story without divulging any specifics might make him more willing to open up to me.

My tactic worked.

He jammed the tack back into the poster with force, twisting it sharply like he was taking out his frustration on the helpless glossy paper. "Join the club."

"If it's any consolation, you're not alone," I offered gently. "It sounds like this was Fox's pattern."

"That's not much help. He tried to ruin me and came fairly close to succeeding."

"Ruin you how?" I wondered if Fox had filmed footage at Theodore's store, too.

"I got a call a couple of months ago from a PR firm representing Fox Andrews and the Headset, although, at the time, I didn't know anything about the Headset. They reached out to me to offer an exclusive partnership to debut Fox's top-secret product at my store. I had to sign an NDA. It was a big deal. I was thrilled. I have a decent local following. We do game nights at the store and that sort of thing, but we've never had a major company contact us about a product launch." He kept massaging the top of his thighs as he spoke.

A nervous habit?

Or was he nervous for another reason?

What I found interesting and slightly odd was that his speech had become stronger and more fluid the longer we spoke.

Was it an act?

I couldn't quite get a read on him.

"I signed the NDA and followed their instructions to the letter. I spent a ton of cash I didn't have to prepare for the event. They were supposed to send posters, fliers, and extra materials, but it was my job to ready the store. They anticipated we could have upwards of two hundred people. I rented chairs and extra tables. I completely rearranged the space in order to accommodate big crowds. I was told the press would be showing up, so I gave the shop a fresh coat of paint and brought some of my most valuable collectibles to display. I advertised to my mailing list and with the local papers. A friend owns a cupcake shop, and I decided to splurge and order custom cupcakes from her. I figured it would be good branding for the store."

"That's a great idea."

He scowled and punched his fist into his palm. "It would have been, except they canceled on me."

"They canceled?" The more I learned about Fox Andrews, the clearer it became that his business practices were less than ethical. The question was, had those business practices led to his murder? Could Theodore or Laurel have killed him because of the detrimental impact he'd had on their stores?

"Not just canceled, but canceled an hour into the event. I had a line wrapped around the block of eager customers waiting to get in and try out the Headset. Three local news stations sent reporters and camera crews. It was a total disaster. At first, I thought maybe Fox was late. Isn't that a thing? You're supposed to be fashionably late to a party?"

I wasn't sure that rule applied to a product launch, especially if the press were involved, but I let him continue.

"I called and texted his PR people. They ghosted me. I should have figured it out when the posters and fliers, let alone the Headset, never arrived. When I finally heard back from the PR woman, she said there had been a last-minute product glitch, and it wasn't ready for the market. I explained that I had over a hundred people at my store waiting to meet Fox. If nothing else, he could have shown and hyped everyone about the product, but he didn't even bother to come."

"What did you do?" A wave of buzzy energy spread down

my arms. I felt like I was getting a clearer picture of Fox and growing more confident that there were several conference attendees with a motive to kill him.

"What could I do?" He threw his hands up. "I had to tell everyone the launch was off. People accused me of making it up. They thought it was a stunt to get people into the store. All of my time and money were down the drain, and I had nothing to show for it."

"Did you ask the PR firm about rescheduling?"

"That's the first thing I asked. They said their timeline had changed, and they were making other arrangements. They wouldn't even reimburse me for the costs of the rental chairs and tables, cupcakes, or my marketing expenses."

As with Laurel, I felt empathy for him and his situation, but in no way was I ready to remove his name from my list of potential suspects.

"I couldn't believe it when I received my panel assignment for the convention, and Fox was one of the panelists." He nodded to a guy dressed as Deadpool, who squeezed by us to get in line for the comic book signing.

I waited for Deadpool to pass before I continued. "Had you spoken with him?"

"No. I never spoke with him. We met for the first time right before the panel. Everything was through his 'people.'"

"Did you ask him about canceling when you met today?"

"I didn't have a chance. I was planning to after the panel, but now he's dead." Theodore shrugged, sounding less than fazed by the fact that he'd witnessed his fellow panelist's death right in front of his eyes. "I guess that's karma."

I kept my face neutral, but I wasn't sure I agreed on that definition of karma. That was a cold response to say the least.

"Fox won't be able to ruin another small shop again." He motioned to the signing table where the line had died down to let the artists know he'd be right over. "It looks like I'm needed."

"You wanted to ask me something?" I nudged.

"Yeah, right. Um, I was curious if you know the police officer in charge." He stared at his feet as he spoke.

"Detective Greene?" I offered.

"Yeah, her." He looked up, his face brightening a little. "You said you were a private detective, right?"

"That's correct." I nodded.

"Like I mentioned, she seems to be clued into me for some reason, and if you're a private eye, maybe you can help me." His voice took on a pleading, hopeful tone.

I was curious where he was going with this. "How?"

"I think something weird was going on between Fox and Victor Moore."

"Really. Like what?" This was a new piece of information I hadn't been expecting.

"I can't say for sure, but I heard them backstage before our panel. It was intense. They were fighting about something. It sounded like Victor was accusing Fox of stealing his technology. He threatened him. He's the guy the police should be investigating."

"Good to know." My heart ticked up a beat. This was another nugget of information that could prove useful.

"Will you look into it?"

"I'll see what I can do." I was glad Fletcher was already on the task of researching Victor Moore and his company. Fletcher's ability to gather information was stellar. I had little doubt he'd have plenty to fill me in on when we met up for happy hour.

"I appreciate it. Thanks." He mopped his brow with the back of his hand and moved toward the signing table. I was pleasantly surprised with how much Laurel and Theodore had shared, but unfortunately, I was nowhere near ready to make a guess as to who had killed Fox.

NINE

To kill time before meeting Fletcher and the others, I listened to the end of a panel with four romance authors discussing ideas for Bookstore Romance Day. I made notes for next year. We didn't carry a huge selection of romances since our primary focus was mysteries, but our Mary Westmacott section was stocked with everything from Jane Austen to Christina Lauren. We'd hosted our first book matchmaking weekend in February, which was wildly popular. Fletcher and I had already been brainstorming ways to expand on the idea.

After the panel, I headed to the bar to find everyone for happy hour.

The hotel bar embraced the midcentury modern aesthetic, featuring a slanted beamed ceiling, painted a crisp white and illuminated with gold accent lighting. Vibrant yellow-and-burnt-orange chairs paired with light wood tables created an inviting contrast. Pops of colorful artwork lined the walls.

The space was humming with activity. Funky postmodern pop played overhead. The bar was packed with attendees queued up for drink specials. I scanned the busy room, looking for my friends, but I didn't have to look far because Pri jumped to her feet and hollered, "Annie! Annie Murray, get your beautiful face over here—stat."

I blushed as the people standing near me chuckled at Pri's enthusiastic greeting.

Pri had scored seats at the coveted book nook. She looked like she belonged on a chaise longue somewhere in the Greek Isles with her flowing silk tangerine pants, strappy sandals, and cream tank top. Her long, dark hair fell to her shoulders in soft waves, and she accentuated her outfit with teal and gold jewelry.

"You look like a pool goddess," I said, giving her a long hug. "We should be outside."

"That's me. Goddess of the sea." She did a little spin, stretching out one arm to pose for me, and winked. "And no way. This is so adorable. All the touches—the book stacks, the mood lighting, these cozy chairs. It even smells like a library in here. I couldn't figure it out. Like are they piping in the book smell somehow?"

I laughed and breathed deeply. She wasn't wrong. There was a distinct, almost smoky aroma in the bar. "Uh, maybe."

"No, they are." She gestured to the bar. "Fletcher's going to lose his ever-loving mind. They're doing a Baskerville Fog as one of the specials. It's a bourbon-based cocktail with lapsang tea that's served under a dome of smoke. So clever and so aromatic." She inhaled through her nostrils like a yoga instructor modeling deep-breathing techniques.

"I love it," I said. "Let me tell you, I'm so happy to see you. It's been a day."

"Sit. Sit." She motioned to one of the cushy armchairs. "Liam's getting us drinks."

My heart skipped a beat at his name. Even though we'd been dating for months, I still felt fluttery whenever he was near. We'd been growing even closer. He'd finally opened up to me about his past and had championed my investigation into

Scarlet's murder. We also had so much fun together—Sunday-morning hikes through the coastal redwoods followed by home-made sourdough pancakes, game night with Pri and Penny, and beer tasting at the Stag Head. I couldn't believe how seamlessly he'd become such an integral part of my life.

"I've already heard some chatter." Pri swept her hand toward the crowded bar and leaned closer, dropping her voice. "An accident, or was it murder?"

I nibbled on the inside of my cheek. "It looks like murder."

Her mouth hung open. "Seriously, Annie. What are the odds?"

"I don't want to know." I was about to fill her in on the details when Liam appeared. He deftly balanced four glasses thanks to his years tending bar. He was dressed in a pair of light khaki slacks and a sky-blue button-up shirt that made his skin look like it had been dipped in bronze. His hair was naturally streaked with subtle highlights from the summer sun and fell over the side of his face.

"Hey, Murray." He caught my eye and let his gaze linger for a minute. Then he set the drinks on the table and pulled me toward him for a kiss.

I wanted nothing more than to collapse in his strong arms and forget about Fox's murder. Liam had a naturally calming and solid presence. And he always smelled good—like a mix of the redwoods and freshly baked bread. I breathed in deeply as he released me.

"It sounds like you could use a cocktail, and ironically or unironically, I got you the Red Herring." He sat next to me and wrapped his arm around the back of my chair. "It's a strawberry daquiri with a surprise kick of spice."

"I'm still trying to make sense of what happened," I admitted, reaching for the pretty pink drink.

"Do you want to talk about it or need a break?" Pri asked,

running her teeth over her bottom lip. "If you just want to chill, I get it."

I appreciated her concern, but I wanted their input, and I'd found that the more I broke down what I'd learned from suspects, the easier it was to see holes in their story or pick up on pieces of information that I missed.

"No, I need to rehash it." I lifted my glass and checked to see if Fletcher was around. "Fletcher should be here soon. Hopefully, he'll have more to add. We decided to divide and conquer." I spotted him. "Oh, there he is now. Perfect." I didn't want to repeat everything I told Pri and Liam or leave Fletcher out of the conversation.

"Greetings. Greetings." He circled his hand with a flourish. "Have I missed much?"

"Not at all," I replied. "I just sat down, and Liam brought us drinks."

"They knew you were coming, Fletcher." Liam passed him the drink with its smoky glass dome. "I give you the Baskerville Fog."

"Thank you. I'll toast to that." Fletcher arranged his jacket on the chair. Then, he proceeded to lift the dome, carefully revealing a cloud of smoke. "You're right, it's like they know me. I feel seen." He blew the smoke away and turned to me. "Annie, would you like to enlighten us with what you've discovered first, or shall I relay the gory details of my research?"

I couldn't believe he had made it all day in the scarf. I had to give him credit for his commitment.

"Gory research details, please." Pri rubbed her hands together.

A smile tugged at the sides of Fletcher's lips as he took a long sip of his cocktail. "Has Annie given you the overview?"

I shook my head. "They've only heard rumors thus far."

"I'll start from the beginning, then." Fletcher crossed one leg over the other and got comfortable. After relaying the basic details of Fox's death, he explained that he snuck off to his room to do some digging into Victor Moore and the Read Moore e-reader. "The concept is quite ingenious. The Read Moore registers eye movements to optimize the perfect TBR list."

"I'm going to take heat for this, but what's a TRB list?" Liam asked, bracing himself in anticipation of getting slugged by Fletcher or Pri.

"Uh, that's TBR—to be read, obviously." Pri rolled her eyes. "Liam Donovan, I'm disappointed in you. Severely disappointed."

"I knew that." He gave us a cheeky grin. "I just wanted to see what you would do. Come on, Annie's trained me better than that. I can't believe you fell for it."

Pri punched him lightly on the shoulder. "I'm keeping an eye on you this weekend, Donovan."

It was sweet to see their friendship and connection continue to develop. Liam's teasing and banter had attracted me to him in the first place, and knowing that he and Pri were tight made me fall even harder.

"Let's get back to the murder, yes?" Fletcher lifted one eyebrow and tapped his phone screen. "As I was saying, the Read Moore technology is revolutionary, but the application leaves room for improvement."

"Is it on the market yet, or is Victor debuting it here like Fox?" I asked.

"Victor did a soft launch last month. A few bookstores are carrying the product, but the reviews are abysmal." Fletcher handed me his phone. "Take a look for yourself."

I scanned through reviews. The consensus seemed to be that no one understood the intended use of the Read Moore.

I read one of the reviews out loud. "This sums it up concisely. 'Is it a sleek new e-reader or a cool party trick that your eye movements auto-load your dream reading list?'"

"I do enjoy a cool party trick," Pri said, leaning closer to get a better look at Fletcher's phone.

"Who doesn't?" Fletcher agreed, keeping his voice low as more people packed into the already crowded bar. "The reviews aren't even exactly negative. It's more that readers are confused with the Read Moore's intention. It's very vague. It's a hard sell to ask a reader to spend close to a hundred dollars on a product they have no idea what to do with."

"We're in the heart of Silicon Valley," Liam said, glancing toward the lobby. "It sounds like Victor landed venture capital or partnered with a bunch of tech bros and pitched an idea without surveying actual readers to determine if there was a need."

"That's the trend right now." I handed Fletcher his phone. "With AI and such a push for putting out books faster and faster. I can't begin to count how many email and phone solicitations we get at the store these days for everything from book lights that play music and special reading glasses with built-in dictionaries."

"It's a brave new book world." Fletcher tucked his phone in his satchel. "We also get inundated with companies trying to get us to feature their apps instore. It doesn't make sense, but you're right, Annie, Read Moore is another well-funded but poorly executed book product. I wish these companies would ever bother to set foot in a bookstore. I could give them dozens of ideas for technology that could improve the shopping experience, like the back-end inventory system, but instead, they give us things we'll never use."

"I wonder how this might tie in with Fox's murder?" I took a sip of my drink. It was bright and refreshing, with a subtle sweetness from the strawberries and, as promised, a spicy kick of chili powder.

A server stopped at our table with a tray of appetizers. "Help yourselves."

We didn't hesitate to load little plates with bruschetta, spinach, and artichoke puff pastry bites and cute hummus dip cups with skewered vegetables.

"I'm suddenly famished," I said, plunging a carrot into the creamy hummus.

"Me too." Pri popped a tomato in her mouth. "We're still going out to dinner after this, right?"

"Yes. I made a reservation at a restaurant down the street from Silicon Summit Partners," I replied, scooping extra hummus onto the carrot. "It sounds like the staff frequents it, so maybe we'll get lucky tonight and have a chance to eavesdrop."

"Count me in," Fletcher said, taking his veggies off the skewer and piling them neatly on his plate. "As for our current murder, I did find a connection between Fox and Victor." He picked up a red pepper and carefully dunked it into the hummus, holding it by the tip to avoid getting his fingers messy.

"Don't leave us hanging." Pri strummed her fingers on the table. Tiny temporary hand-drawn tattoos ran along her forearms. Her artistry was unparalleled. She had a gift for illustration. I'd once asked her why she'd never made any of her tattoos permanent fixtures on her skin. Her answer made perfect sense —the process of creating art was her happy place. She didn't want to commit to anything that would be forever etched on her but rather wanted to explore new designs and techniques, constantly changing her appearance.

Fletcher chomped the red pepper and nodded. After he finished the bite, he wiped his hands on a napkin and dabbed the sides of his lips. "I discovered an old social media thread between the two of them. Fox posted teasers about the Headset. Victor went after him in the comments, accusing him of stealing his technology. He didn't hold back."

"That came up in the panel," I interrupted. "They had an exchange about stealing tech."

"Fox must have blocked Victor at some point because there

are dozens of comments back and forth, which I'll never under-stand. It's like having a public argument. Do they not realize that everyone is watching?" Fletcher carefully dabbed his lips again with a napkin.

"Sometimes, I think that is *the* reason people post publicly," Liam said with a half frown.

"Agreed. In any event, the comments continued for a few weeks. Victor was the first to post any time Fox shared a photo or video. He didn't self-edit. I took screenshots, which I'll send to you, Annie, and Detective Greene. But then, a couple of weeks ago, Victor vanished from social. Fox had been posting. He was active this morning before he died, but there was no rebuttal from Victor."

"That's why you think Victor was banned from Fox's social channels?" I asked, taking a sip of my Red Herring.

"It's the most logical explanation. It may have taken Fox or his team a while to get Victor banned. Although I am surprised that they didn't hide or delete his earlier comments."

"Controversy sells," Pri said, reaching into her oversized purse and removing a silky wrap in the same tangerine as her pants. She tied it around her shoulders. "I was joking at Cryptic that we should offer something utterly unappetizing on our summer coffee menu for the tourists."

"Like what?" Liam rubbed my arm as he spoke. His subtle show of affection made heat rush to my cheeks.

My fair, freckled skin tends to burn in the sun and turn red and splotchy at the most inopportune times, like now.

"Maybe a grass-infused latte—notes of straw, earthy dirt, and morning dew." She grinned.

"That sounds awful." Fletcher stuck out his tongue.

"Right?" Pri's smile widened. Her eyes lit up mischievously. "That's why it's so brilliant. People will definitely talk about a grass latte. They'll tell their friends, who will have to come sample it for themselves. I'm telling you, controversy sells. It's a genius marketing strategy."

"Yes, but you fail to mention people already drive miles and miles out of their way to come to taste your exquisitely hand-crafted coffees." I tipped my head to the side and raised one eyebrow. "I don't think you need a marketing gimmick. You have a cult coffee following."

"Aw, thanks, Annie. See, I barely had to fish for a compliment." Pri fanned her face like she was blushing. "No, but seriously, I bet Fox left the comments online because controversy generates even more engagement."

I nodded. She had a point, and if Fox had stolen Victor's proprietary technology and used it in the Headset, that gave Victor a strong motive for murder.

TEN

Fletcher finished updating us on his research into Victor Moore, and I filled everyone in on what I'd learned from Theodore and Laurel.

"So basically, all three of them wanted Fox Andrews dead," Pri said, polishing off her cocktail and wrapping her shawl tighter around her arms.

"Yep." I took a final sip of mine, too. "And unfortunately, we have a couple more contenders—Serena Highbourn, a famous tell-all author. She and Fox argued shortly before he died, and she was in the front row. I'm not sure how she could have pulled it off, but there's a chance she could have slipped onto the stage and swapped the Headset before the panel. She was definitely cued into the talk, taking notes on her tablet. However, there could be a simple explanation for that. She is a gossip writer, after all."

"And murder sells even better than controversy," Pri interjected. "You know, I wouldn't mind having a chat with her. I've read a few of her books, and *damn*—she does not hold back. Maybe we'll have to pop into one of her signings in between our coffee tastings tomorrow, Liam."

Liam looked at me for confirmation. "Would that be helpful?"

"Sure. Anything is helpful at this stage. What I don't get about this event is that it's not her usual celebrity gossip, so I can't quite wrap my head around her angle. She's by far the biggest celebrity here. Plus, I still need to speak with Phillip Kaufman, the other panelist. At this point, anyone in the near vicinity of Fox when he was killed is on my list."

"That's a lot of suspects." Liam's brow creased with concern. "Do you want to hang around the hotel longer and try to speak with them, or should we continue to dinner?"

"I vote dinner." I set my empty glass on the low coffee table. "A couple of carrots and hummus are not going to sustain me, and Fletcher and I can continue our inquiries tomorrow. If you two happen to have time to swing by Serena's signings, go for it. The convention runs for three more days. Everyone is on their own for dinner tonight, so tracking down Serena and Phillip might be difficult. Plus, I'm guessing Detective Greene will make an appearance in the morning, so we can relay what we've discovered about the others then."

"You don't have to twist my arm." Pri stuck out her arm for me to twist. "I can always eat."

"Good. The place I found is a progressive Indian-inspired restaurant. I could not stop drooling over the menu. They claim to put a modern spin and interpretation on well-loved classic dishes."

"Let's stop talking about food and go. Eat. Food." Pri pretended to stuff her face.

I chuckled as Liam helped me to my feet. "It's a short walk if you want to stretch your legs. Otherwise, we can carpool."

"A walk sounds nice," Liam said, waiting for me to lead the way.

We cut through the pool courtyard and past the cabanas. Sunlight kissed the rows of lemon and orange trees lining the path. Potted palms and birds of paradise flanked the exit. We turned onto the sidewalk and strolled through a neighborhood of matching midcentury modern houses. The single-story houses with flat roofs and large windows were painted in bold colors—dark gray with a sunflower-yellow front door and navy blue with pumpkin trim. Lawns had been torn up and replaced with native gardens and turf.

"I could live here," Pri said, peering over a half-brick wall. "I think every house in this neighborhood has its own swimming pool."

"I'd hate to see a price tag," Fletcher said, carrying his coat over his arm like a waiter with a crisp white dish towel. "I bet they sell for a few million."

"These are Eichlers," Liam said. "My grandparents owned one when I was young, and now they're coveted. I don't doubt they'd go for a pretty penny."

"I had no idea you were an architecture buff." I squeezed his hand.

"They say that the best architects design with love in mind. I guess that means some buildings like these are meant to last a lifetime." He shot me a knowing look and casually bumped his shoulder against mine. "I do enjoy dabbling in architectural guidebooks now and then, but I'm only familiar with the Eichler design because I loved staying with my grandparents. The entire back of the house has glass sliding doors, bringing the outside in. They're known for the minimalist style and abundant natural light."

"Were your grandparents in the Bay Area?" We'd never spoken much about his family, though recently, he had let his guard down and let me in about his painful history. His long-time girlfriend cheated on him with his brother, and his mom died shortly after they'd run off together. He didn't have much of a relationship with his dad. I was glad he felt comfortable enough to be vulnerable with me, and I'd been gently nudging him to reach out to his brother when he was ready.

"Yeah, not too far from here. I'll drive you by their old place on our way home."

"I'd love that," I said truthfully, dropping his hand briefly to pause and get a closer look at one of the houses. Every new glimpse into Liam's past gave me a better understanding of him. I wondered if he felt the same. I needed to do the same. Soon, it was going to be time to introduce him to my parents. It was a big step, but I was ready.

He strolled ahead just a bit with his hands in his pockets, before turning back to me with a sly grin. "You coming, or are you wrapped up in thinking about how charming I am?"

"Definitely the charm," I said, my voice dripping with light sarcasm. I rolled my eyes but couldn't hide a smile. "You're basically a modern-day Darcy." With a quick step I caught up to him and fell into stride beside him. "Though you could improve on your brooding silence and questionable social skills."

"Challenge accepted." He narrowed his brows and took my hand again.

The restaurant was on the corner of the next block. It was easy to spot with its large wooden pergola draped with greenery and strings of golden twinkle lights. Beneath the canopy of fairy lights and vines, rustic wooden tables paired with benches created a cozy, communal feel. Charming lanterns were scattered throughout the patio, casting a soft, flickering glow.

"Oh, yay, we can sit outside." Pri clapped. "Well, that is if we can get a table. It looks busy."

"I'm one step ahead of you. I made a reservation for outside."

"That's why we love you, Annie. Mad organizational skills."

I laughed. Before we crossed the street, I pointed to a grouping of buildings farther down the block. The main building was a behemoth compared with anything back home on the village square in Redwood Grove. Three stories, constructed of glass and heavy steel, with a long, gated driveway secured by a guard station. "That's the Silicon Summit Partners campus."

"Weird. I expected it to be a big high rise in the middle of downtown, not tucked into a neighborhood," Fletcher said.

"They own ten blocks," I said, gesturing toward the campus. Walking paths wound through carefully manicured lawns just beyond the imposing gate that sealed off the buildings from public access. Neatly trimmed hedges and the occasional decorative fountain gave the appearance of a public park—inviting and serene. But the façade was just that: a façade.

I knew that behind the meticulous landscaping was something far less inviting. The gated entrance wasn't just decorative. The gates were reinforced, monitored, and meant to keep people out. Security cameras were nestled among the trees, tracking everyone from the moment they stepped onto the property.

This was my first time seeing it in person, but I'd reviewed every square inch of the campus layout on blueprints and photos online. "It gives off the vibe of being a welcoming space, but nothing could be further from the truth," I said, keeping my voice down. "Getting in is going to be another story. Everything is locked down. The perimeter is gated, with guards at every entrance. You need a badge to get past the lobby, and that's just the beginning."

"That's why we're here," Liam said. "Dinner is a good opportunity to strategize."

We were seated quickly and ordered one of everything on the menu—butter chicken, lamb shank nihari with rose petals, paneer pinwheels, wild mushroom dosa, and assorted papads and crisps served with chili and peanut chutney and avocado raita.

"I'm glad we're hungry," I said when the food arrived. "This is enough for a small army."

"Speak for yourself." Pri dipped a spoon into the avocado raita. "My grandmother's table looks like this, and I win our family's eating competition every time, so don't pace yourselves."

We chatted as we enjoyed the delectable food infused with layers of spices and sauces that tasted like it'd simmered for days. I was glad for a reprieve from Fox's murder, but I was distracted by people-watching. Anytime the staff seated a group of businesspeople, I half expected to find Logan Ashford staring back at me.

"Are you thinking about Scarlet?" Liam whispered as he passed me a basket of papads.

"How are you such a mind reader?" I swallowed the lump forming in my throat as I thought about the task in front of us. The reality of being here now made it feel all the more daunting.

"Bartending, it comes with the territory. Customers linger at the bar and bare their souls."

"Of course." I felt bad that I was so obvious, but this was the closest I'd been to Scarlet in years. The last place she'd visited before she died was Silicon Summit Partners. We were mere blocks away. Part of me wanted to sprint down the street, force my way in, and confront Logan this very instant.

"Is Annie baring her soul?" Fletcher asked, cutting his butter chicken with a fork and a knife.

The tender meat practically melted in my mouth. "No, I was just thinking that I wish there was another way in, but I think it has to be me."

"Can I, once again, put it on record that I disagree?" Liam scowled.

"I hate to say it, but I agree," Pri said. "It feels too danger- ous. Logan might be a criminal, but he's a smart one. What are the odds he's going to believe after all these years you've had a change of heart and want to work with him?"

"Not with him, *for* him. I agree; it's dangerous. The one thing I can say is I have rehearsed my cover story to the point that I believe it." Tiny fireworks exploded in my stomach as I imagined sitting in front of Logan, seeing his face in person for the first time.

Pri stabbed a mushroom with her fork. "Do it again. For me."

I felt like an actor getting notes from her director. Pri had heard my pitch at least ten times. She could probably recite it as well as me, but there was no harm in running through it again. "Logan, you might not know me, but you knew my roommate and best friend, Scarlet."

"Pause for an awkward gasp, followed by a quick recovery," Fletcher said, holding up his palms and pressing his lips together.

"What if he kicks you out right then?" Liam asked.

"He won't. He'll want to know what I know. I'm sure he's already well aware of my meeting with Mark, and I'm equally convinced he hired Elspeth to try and kill me. Plus, I've flooded his inbox with emails and left him dozens of voicemails. He knows who I am and what I'm up to. He's going to want to talk to me, if for nothing else than to figure out if I have anything substantial on him."

"Another reason this isn't a good idea," Liam huffed under his breath but caught himself. "Sorry, continue."

"I'll gauge his response as I go. Then I'll follow up by revealing that I recently discovered new information about Scarlet's death and her employment contract with the company. I'll explain that I've been barely scraping by at the bookstore, and revisiting Scarlet's case has prompted me to return to my roots. That's when I break out Fletcher's magnum opus and go in for the kill. I need to convince him he has a mole and his security is threatened. I'll show him my private detective's license and beg him for an opportunity to work for him."

"You really think he's going to buy it?" Pri sounded skeptical as her brows tugged into a frown.

"No. I doubt he'll buy it at all, but that's not the goal. The goal is to get in. I just have to get in there. He's already nervous. We know that much. I'm his last loose end, but he can't risk killing me. I've been too public about Scarlet. Not to mention Dr. Caldwell. He knows we're back in contact. Like you said, Pri, he's not stupid. He's gotten away with extortion and murder for years. He doesn't want to lose everything he has. No, I'm confident he'll agree because he can keep an eye on me." The fiery feeling returned, sending sparks from the top of my head to the tips of my toes. This had to work. There was no other way.

Fletcher folded his napkin into a neat square. It never ceased to amaze me how he could be so fastidious with his appearance and personal grooming, and yet his side of our shared office always looked like it had been hit by a tornado. "What's the plan after you're in, so to speak?"

"I need to get to Human Resources. Assuming everything goes smoothly, he'll send me to HR for paperwork. I'm going to have to wing it from there, depending on how he reacts." What I didn't say out loud was that this was the part of the plan that still had some gaping holes—like how to find the evidence.

"We could *Mission: Impossible* this. You could spike the HR director's tea with a laxative," Fletcher suggested. "Steal the keys, lock everyone out of the building, and start your search. Something like that?"

I laughed. "Somehow, I think that might go disastrously wrong. It won't be easy, but I need to get my hands on Natalie's evidence."

"Assuming they haven't found it and shredded it." Liam raised his eyebrows in a challenging stare. "You're sure it's still there? It's been years, Annie. I mean, don't get me wrong, I fully support you in this mission, but there is a decent chance that whatever Natalie hid before she made her escape is long gone."

"I know." I sighed, feeling the familiar rumble of nerves spread through my body.

"Wouldn't the police have searched the building years ago when they assumed she was dead?" Pri raised yet another question I'd asked myself.

"Yes." I nodded, feeling my pulse tick up. "They swept the entire building, but no one other than her and Scarlet knew about it. The police wouldn't have been looking for documents or a hidden folder they didn't even know existed. If Scarlet found it, I'm sure it's still there. She was smart and cunning. She would have had a plan. There's no chance she would have confronted Logan with the evidence in hand. She was smarter than that. She loved puzzles and Clue and anything secret. I'm sure it's there. I just have to figure out where."

"True. All right, okay, best-case scenario, Logan buys your story, or at least goes along with it for his own nefarious purposes, you land a date with HR, then what?" Liam refilled our water glasses.

"Then I wing it. I use the skills I've honed for the last decade. If I can get in, I trust myself. I will find the files—I'll do whatever it takes."

"That I believe." Fletcher raised his glass in a toast to me. "Meanwhile, we'll be waiting and watching, ready to call the cavalry."

"I'll have a direct line to Dr. Caldwell the entire time," Pri said seriously.

"Tomorrow?" Liam asked, meeting my gaze. His eyes were flecked with gold and worry.

"Tomorrow." I nodded. I was ready. It was time to meet Logan face-to-face. And make him pay.

ELEVEN

The next morning, I woke up early and decided to swim before breakfast. The pool was empty. Pinkish morning light skirted across the deck, illuminating the crystal-clear waters. Golden finches and hummingbirds flitted between the potted succulents and swaths of pink jasmine.

The rhythm of my strokes cutting through the water was like a meditation. There was something oddly comforting about the scent of sunscreen mingling with chlorine. With each lap, I felt clearer and more resolved for my meeting with Logan Ashford. It was almost like Scarlet was swimming beside me, urging me on. I could do this. I had to do this.

Afterwards, I took a leisurely shower and got ready for the day. I chose a flared spring skirt with dainty wildflowers, a V-neck shirt, and a cardigan. My pale purple glasses and earrings finished the bookish look. I wanted to be professional for the conference and also appear casual—like a bookseller—when I met with Logan. Anything I could do to come across as unassuming would benefit me. I wanted him to think he had the upper hand.

Pri and Liam were already off on a coffee-tasting adventure.

They mapped out a dozen local coffee shops they wanted to visit for inspiration for Cryptic and the Stag Head. I wasn't sure how coffee culture might translate to Liam's rustic bar. I had a feeling he was tagging along to keep Pri company. If he was trying to make me fall harder for him, it was working.

"Pace yourself," I cautioned when he left before my swim. "That's a lot of potential caffeine. Maybe you can go decaf after the first few shops."

"Decaf? Never." His hair fell over his eye as he shook his head. "Pri would disown me. Can you imagine?"

"True, but how are you going to consume twelve—or more—cups of coffee?"

"I have my ways, Murray. I have my ways." He kissed the top of my head. "I'll see you later, fully caffeinated."

The thought of a strong cup of coffee pulled me back into the present. I checked my appearance one last time. My reddish hair had a natural wave thanks to the pool and humidity. I added a touch of blush and lip gloss, grabbed my tote bag, and headed downstairs to the convention.

The lobby was already bustling with booksellers eager for another day of panels, signings, and shopping. Tables with carafes of freshly brewed coffee, pastries, fruit, and juices called to me. I was suddenly famished. Before I could fill my plate, I heard someone calling my name. "Hey, Annie, do you have a minute?"

I turned to see Detective Greene flagging me down. She stood at a high-top table, nursing a black cup of coffee. "You're here early."

She checked her smartwatch. "Someone is late and I'm not happy about it. Serena Highbourn was supposed to be here twenty minutes ago."

It was a bold move not to show up for a meeting with the police. Then again, I got the sense that Serena Highbourn was used to people catering to her, not the other way around.

"Get some coffee and a pastry," Detective Greene said, motioning to the long tables. "I'd love to hear if you have any new information for me, but I don't want to hold up your breakfast."

"I have quite a bit to share, but I won't turn down coffee. I'll be right back." I hurried to join the short line. The crowd was sparse. Panels didn't start for another forty minutes, so I guessed people would trickle in shortly. I poured a cup of coffee with a splash of oat milk and surveyed the food options. Pineapple, cantaloupe, and grapes were arranged in a cascade of fruit. There were berries, yogurt, granola, mouth-watering pastries, and hot items—eggs, bacon, and sausage.

Swimming always made me hungrier than usual. I piled a plate with fruit, an almond bear claw pastry, eggs, and two slices of bacon and returned to Detective Greene.

"You're tempting me to go back for seconds." She nodded to her empty plate. "I wasn't intending to have breakfast, but the organizers encouraged me to try the bear claw. It is exquisite."

"Yum. I swam this morning, and anytime I get out of the pool, I'm ravenous." I broke off a piece of the sweet pastry.

She reached under the table and pulled out a gorgeous, deep-red, hardcover book with sprayed gold edges and an embossed foil cover. "Don't tell, but I took a quick detour into the book room and scored this. Isn't she a beauty?"

It was a reprint of Daphne du Maurier's *Rebecca*. "I read this in high school and fell in love with it instantly." She picked up the copy, cradling it like a newborn.

"The company that does these reprints is amazing," I said, examining the book from afar, not wanting to smudge it with sticky fingers. "We can't keep them in the store. Lucky you."

She tucked it carefully into her bag and clapped twice. "I know. I can't wait for a chunk of time off to come visit the Secret Bookcase."

"I'll give you the full Redwood Grove tour."

"I will take you up on that." She opened her notebook and turned to a new page, returning her focus to the investigation. "You mentioned new information?"

I savored the nutty almond filling and soft, buttery crust, washing it down with a sip of coffee. "Yes. I spoke with Theodore Calodin and Laurel Deters. I'm not sure if this will be new information for you, but they both have a history with Fox Andrews." I told her about how Fox shot footage of Laurel's store and bailed on his product debut at Theodore's shop. "Neither of them had good things to say about Fox."

She made notes and asked me a few follow-up questions, stopping twice to remove her phone from her crossbody bag and check her messages. "This matches what we've heard."

"Are you aware of Victor Moore's history with his Read Moore technology?" I popped a juicy grape in my mouth.

"Our team has been digging into every angle—personal lives, business dealings, financial records. If there's something buried in any of the suspects' pasts, we'll find it."

"I don't think Victor's buried much." I took a bite of the eggs and bacon and explained his claim that Fox had stolen his technology and about the comments Fletcher had found online.

"This is very helpful. Thank you." She ran her finger along the rim of her coffee. "You didn't have a chance to speak with Serena Highbourn by chance?"

"No. I didn't see her again. I don't know if she left."

"She better not have left. Everyone is under strict orders not to leave town without our permission."

"I doubt Serena follows orders." I was about to say more when the bestselling author swept into the lobby, intentionally causing a scene. "Speak of the devil."

Detective Greene swiveled her head.

Serena glided through the room like a queen greeting her loyal subjects. She wiggled her bejeweled fingers in little waves as she passed by tables, nodding as if bestowing gifts upon everyone by simply gracing us with her presence. "Officer, many apologies. I was a tad delayed in preparing for this morning. It takes a team to get my face looking like this." She tipped her chin and placed her hand on her cheek.

I hadn't noticed yesterday, but in this unforgiving morning light and at this distance, her makeup looked like it had been applied for a stage production. The foundation was so heavy it created an artificial mask, blurring the lines between her real skin and the painted perfection. Layers of powder and pigment clung to her face, hiding every pore and any hint of natural texture. It was impossible to tell where the makeup ended and she began.

I couldn't help wondering if she was trying to conceal something else.

She removed her earbuds, fidgeted with the silver and gold bangles on her wrists, pushing them up her thin arms, and stared at me with newfound interest. "I don't think we've been formally introduced." She extended a limp hand.

I wasn't sure if she wanted me to shake or kiss it. I gave her a wave instead. "I'm Annie Murray. We met yesterday. At the panel."

"Yes, of course. You did a marvelous job." She tapped Detective Greene's sleeve. "You should give her a raise. She was brilliant. Jumped on stage and took charge."

"I don't work for the police. I explained that yesterday." Was Serena so self-absorbed that she hadn't listened to anything I said, or was this part of her larger-than-life author persona? Either way, I wasn't fond of her affected speech or condescending attitude.

"Annie is assisting us." Detective Greene gave me a knowing look. "In fact, I'd appreciate it if you could stay."

"Sure." I nodded, watching to gauge Serena's reaction.

Serena flinched ever so slightly but hid it quickly. She placed her headphones into their case and then pressed her fingers together and rested her elbows on the table. "My publicist should be arriving any moment. I have hundreds of books to sign, so if we could speed this along, that would be wonderful."

"Tell us about your relationship with Fox Andrews," Detective Greene asked, waiting with her pen in hand.

"What is there to know? I suppose you could say we were casual acquaintances. His people contacted my people and wanted me to lend my name to the Headset. They thought it would pull in a new audience if I recommended the device. I politely declined. I haven't the faintest interest in this new-fangled technology, and, please, I've sold millions of copies worldwide. My books have been translated into eighty languages. An endorsement from me would indeed attract a large audience for him, but what's in it for me? My readership wants the juicy Hollywood and royalty gossip. They don't need a virtual reality experience."

"Fox wanted to create VR experiences based on your tell-alls? How would that even work?" I asked.

Detective Greene nodded to show she was on the same page.

"Honey, I have no idea. Fox Andrews was delusional. He went so far as to suggest that he could reach out to my client base directly. Not likely. It's taken me years to build my reputation as a trusted source. Who's going to air their dirty laundry to a scrawny nobody? People underestimate how much relationship-building goes into my job. You have to look the part." She ran her arm over her expensive cream suit. "Hollywood speaks to Hollywood. The royals 'leak' stories to their most trusted sources, like me." She used air quotes to emphasize the word "leak."

"How did he respond when you turned him down?" Detective Greene asked.

"Why would I care? He didn't stand a chance. If he wanted to succeed, he should have put in the work. I didn't become a bestseller overnight. I didn't start with A-list celebrities on speed dial. Oh, I'm dating myself with you two, aren't I? Let's just say you could toss out any name, and the odds are good that they're in my contacts. Shall we try? A royal, perhaps?"

"That's not necessary." Detective Greene cut her off. "Were you surprised to see Fox here at the convention?"

"Nothing surprises me, honey. I've seen and heard it all." She tossed her glossy curls over her shoulder. "Nothing gets by me. Nothing. My methods for extracting gossip are flawless."

I wondered again exactly how Serena went about collecting gossip. Inside sources? Hoarding secrets to use against celebrities? Listening devices?

"Did you interact with him?" Detective Greene wasn't falling for Serena's attempt to flex about how many celebrities she knew. It made me like her even more.

"Briefly. He tried to pitch me again. I explained I didn't have time to hear another desperate plea and that my answer was still no."

"Yet, you were in attendance at his panel."

Serena tossed her hair in the other direction. "I had a few minutes before my signing. I wanted to see if he'd made any gains since he pitched me."

"What kind of gains?" Detective Greene sounded casual, but I had a feeling the question was intentional. If Serena had no interest in endorsing the Headset or technology in general, why attend the panel?

"The demo they sent me was sloppy at best—grainy, bumpy footage. It triggered a migraine. I was curious if he had fixed the glitches."

"Had he?" Detective Greene tapped her pen on the notebook twice.

"How would I know? He died." Serena spoke matter-of-factly without a trace of emotion. Her gaze drifted around the room like she was done with the conversation and eager to find someone else to distract her. "Are we done? I have another signing scheduled. It's terribly rude to leave my public waiting."

"Not yet." Detective Greene flipped to the front of her notebook. "What are you working on now?"

"Nice try. Nope. No. No." Serena shook a finger at Detective Greene. "I never divulge details of my current work in progress. I can't risk any leaks. These are high-profile clients, sharing extremely private information. They expect complete anonymity and discretion."

"These are extenuating circumstances." Detective Greene wasn't taking any of Serena's attitude, and I loved watching her hold her ground. "I'm investigating a murder."

"Murder!" Serena gasped, tossing her hand over her mouth in shock. "My publicist didn't say anything about murder. He was murdered? Fox? Who would want to murder him?"

"That's what we're here to find out." Detective Greene stated the obvious.

I observed Serena. Her reaction seemed theatrical, almost rehearsed. Maybe the stage makeup was throwing me off.

"No, I don't buy it. I was in the front row. The Headset malfunctioned. I told you the demo he sent to me was seizure-inducing. I couldn't keep it on for more than a minute, and then I ended up with a searing migraine for the remainder of the day. I wouldn't be wasting your time with us, Officer; I would be having your lab examine every inch of that worthless product."

"It's Detective," she corrected. "Thanks for the suggestion."

Serena didn't pick up on Detective Greene's sarcasm. "You're welcome. I've been around the block with notorious criminals. I understand how the justice system works."

Detective Greene ignored her comment. "Back to your current project."

"No. Again. No. If you want that information, you'll have to go through my legal team. I have ironclad NDAs that I'm not willing to break, even for a murder investigation."

"I'll be in touch then." Detective Greene closed the notebook.

Serena flitted away.

When she was out of earshot, Detective Greene turned to me and asked, "What's your take?"

"It's hard to say; everything about her is fake and utterly dramatic. We didn't get the whole truth, but I'm not sure if that's because of her incredible ego or if there's more to the story where she and Fox are concerned."

"My thoughts exactly."

"Have you considered having the lab analyze the Headset?" I grinned and made a goofy face.

"No. Such a revolutionary idea. Why didn't I think of it? I'll get right on that." Her face looked even younger when she laughed. "Keep an eye on her, okay?"

"Will do." Serena's lack of technological knowledge made her less likely to be the killer, but had she left out critical pieces of information? Could Fox have gone after her client list? It didn't seem like a hard sell for celebrities to get more airtime. If he was encroaching on her territory, could that have set her on a path toward murder?

TWELVE

Fletcher caught me on my way into the showroom. He was pacing from the coffee table to the door of the convention hall. "Annie, I've been looking everywhere for you."

"Hey! Sorry. I was with Detective Greene." My voice softened as I glanced up at him, guilt creeping in. I hesitated before I shifted my weight and brushed a speck of lint off my sleeve.

"Any updates with the investigation?" His voice was clipped and breathless. "I got worried when you didn't show..." He trailed off.

I swallowed, adjusting my glasses, feeling the weight of his concern sink in. "I'm so sorry. Detective Greene grabbed me when I was getting breakfast, and then I was caught up with her. I should have texted you." I reached for his hand and squeezed it tight to reassure him I was fine. "As for the case, not much yet, except she had me stick around while she questioned Serena Highbourn. I have more questions than answers, but I don't trust Serena. And, wow, can you say high maintenance? She is—" I paused, searching for the right word. "Let's just say she thinks very highly of herself."

"I don't trust any of the people on our suspect list," Fletcher said. He was dressed in slacks and a tailored white shirt with a black crow pattern. A red rose was tucked into his lapel. "I ended up sharing a table with Theodore at breakfast. His story is full of holes—gaping holes."

"Really, like what?" I moved to the side to make room for a vendor wheeling a cart of book journals into the showroom.

"Did you know he wasn't supposed to moderate yesterday's panel? Apparently, a gaming buddy of his is on the board for the convention, and he got Theodore reassigned to moderate the panel at the last minute."

"No, Theodore told me he was invited to moderate and then was shocked to learn that Fox was on the panel."

"That's not what he said at breakfast." Fletcher twisted his lips in an accusatory scowl. "He has no idea that you and I are partners. It's interesting that he shared an entirely different version of how he ended up on the panel with me, isn't it?"

"Did Fox come up?" I peeked into the vendor hall, which was buzzing with activity.

"Oh yeah. He said his friend got him on the panel because he knew Fox had done him dirty. Let me clarify, those were his words, not mine." He raised his brows twice and squeezed his lips into a frown.

"I figured." I chuckled. Fletcher was nothing if not proper when it came to his use of the English language. He would have fit seamlessly into Victorian times with his adoration of the works of Arthur Conan Doyle, his addiction to solving puzzles and crimes, and his fastidious fashion choices.

"Theodore was upfront about it. He told me he was furious with Fox and wanted a chance to have a face-to-face, man-to-man talk. Overkill if you ask me, but I didn't address his grammatical choices in the moment."

"Probably wise." I winked and nodded. "So he went out of his way to be assigned to moderate the panel. I wonder what else he could have concocted in terms of plans for his face-to-face with Fox?"

"We had two divergent conversations. He wasn't shy about his loathing for Fox Andrews." Fletcher fixed his rose boutonniere and checked his watch.

"Did he say anything about the launch event and Fox not showing up?"

"Yes, everything regarding the failed product launch party was verbatim what he told you, but then he became very candid about what a weasel and cheat Fox was and how he was glad to be at the convention to carry out his vendetta."

"Did he use the word 'vendetta'?"

Fletcher sucked his cheeks in as he flashed a peace sign. "Twice."

"Okay, well, that changes things. Theodore is already on my radar, but going out of his way to get assigned to the panel is concerning."

"While we were eating, one of his customers came over to thank him profusely for fixing her laptop. Didn't he claim not to be tech-savvy?"

"He did." That was two lies for Theodore thus far. What else was he lying about?

"I hate to say it, but he's on the top of my list for now." Fletcher reached into his pocket and pulled out a flier. "He gave me this. He's hosting a gaming meetup later this evening. It's invite-only, so I'll try to stop in and see what else I might be able to learn. Obviously, Operation Silicon Summit takes precedence, so only if time allows."

"Great idea. I'm sure there will be time. Where are you off to next, and when is Victoria due to arrive?" Fletcher's girlfriend was on her way to the convention, hence the rose and dapper outfit.

"Hopefully, within the hour. I thought I might peruse products for the store while I wait for her." He pointed to the showroom. "There's nothing I'm excited about until the murder panel."

"The murder panel takes on new meaning since we've had a real murder." The panel featured four California mystery writers. I was eager to hear them speak about our fall event lineup. "I'll come with you. I haven't had a chance to check out any of the vendor booths yet."

"After you, Watson." He ushered me into the showroom.

My eyes didn't know where to land. They darted from one colorful display to the next. Booths stretched out in neat, long rows, each vying for my attention. Some had gone all out, constructing elaborate displays with tents, lights, and life-size banners. Others took a more subtle approach, draping their tables with simple, colorful tablecloths that allowed their books to be the star of the show. Along the perimeter, authors sat at tables with stacks of their latest releases waiting to be signed. Meeting authors was always the highlight of conferences for me. It was a chance to learn more about their process and upcoming works and hopefully entice them to the Secret Bookcase for a signing or special event.

The showroom reminded me of a book fair for adults. When I was young, book-fair days at school were always my favorite. I would save up my allowance and birthday and holiday money and spend hours poring over the book choices in the newsprint catalog. I distinctly remember the eager excitement of stepping into the school library and seeing it transformed with glorious shelves of books waiting to be taken home.

"I'm going to hit the signing tables before the lines get too long," I said, motioning in that direction. I could use a bookish distraction for a few minutes. Dr. Caldwell used to lecture about the importance of taking a break and stepping away from a case to gain perspective. I needed a new perspective on Fox's murder as well as a clue or some kind of guidance from Scarlet about where she might have stashed the evidence.

He checked his watch and scanned the room. "I told Victoria I would help her set up the Book Bus table, but she hasn't texted yet."

"Don't worry about it. You should wait for her. I'll chat with the authors and find you both when I'm done. Tell her hello from me. I'm excited to see her. It's been a while." Fletcher and Victoria had been dating long-distance since Valentine's Day. She recently launched Book Bus, her traveling bookmobile, and from what Fletcher shared, it sounded like it was off to a great start.

"It's been fifteen days exactly," Fletcher replied, tapping his watch.

"But you're not counting?" I teased.

"Not in the slightest."

"Here's to a happy reunion. See you shortly." I left him pacing eagerly by the entrance and headed to the first author's table. She wrote a long-running, popular romantic suspense series. We'd tried to schedule a signing at the Secret Bookcase with her publicist several times, but it hadn't worked with her travel. I was determined to get her on the calendar for our next Mystery Fest in the fall. Luckily, I didn't have to twist her arm. When I introduced myself, she jumped to her feet. "Oh my goodness. I've heard so many amazing things about last year's event and have wanted to visit the store forever. I would love to attend. In fact, I told my publicist to block out any travel until we heard whether it might be possible to be a featured author this year."

I was glad the feeling was mutual and told her we'd be in touch with more details. I left her table with a bag of signed books and my first secured author for our second annual Mystery Fest. Fletcher and I had big plans to expand and grow the festival. Hopefully, the authors on the mystery panel would also be game to join us. Our goal was to have at least five or six authors for the weekend, but ten would be even better.

I wandered from table to table, chatting with authors who wrote everything from sci-fi to nonfiction and letting my mind sink into thoughts about the bookstore, giving it a much-needed break from murder. We predominately carried mysteries at the Secret Bookcase, but I picked up some titles for Liam—he was a huge fan of historical fiction and biographies—as well as books for our children's section and other genre fiction we could display in the Foyer, where we featured a rotation of mysteries and non-mysteries.

Fletcher had floated the idea that we could do a major over-haul of each of the rooms in the bookstore. Instead of focusing solely on mysteries, he suggested we transform each space into dedicated genre fiction rooms. Sci-fi in the Parlor, book club fiction in the Sitting Room, and so forth. We toyed with the concept for about five minutes before abandoning it. There was something uniquely special about a mystery bookshop. We felt that, and our customers did, too. We wanted to put our own touches on the store but not turn it into something unrecognizable.

After I'd had a chance to meet the authors, I wound my way through the vendor booths. There was so much to see. It was sensory overload in the best bookish way—handmade stickers, bookmarks, book charms, journals, calendars, notecards, wrapping paper, plush pillows, and cashmere blankets. The showroom was a booklover's delight. I made notes about products to order and filled my tote with catalogs and fliers for discounts.

"Annie, hi! Oh, good. I was hoping to bump into you this morning." A voice sounded next to me. I turned to see Laurel precariously balancing a tower of books in one arm and a cup of tea in the other. Four bulging tote bags hung from her shoulder, their weight tugging her down. It was a miracle she hadn't spilled the tea.

"Hey, can I lend you a hand?" I reached to catch the tippy stack.

"That would be lovely, thank you, dear. I got a bit carried away. If you wouldn't mind, my room is right down the hall." She tried to point that way, but she could barely lift her arm under the weight of the totes.

"Of course." I let her lead the way. "Are you enjoying the convention?"

"It's even better than I imagined. The only problem is I want to buy everything for the store, but I'll go broke. How do you pace yourself?" She wore practical tennis shoes, a pair of capris and a summer cardigan.

"It's a challenge. Fletcher and I have different tastes, which is helpful. We spend an afternoon after the convention making lists of our favorites. Whenever we land on products we both love, we put those on the top. Then some of it is trial and error. Sometimes, things we're sure are going to fly off the shelves sit for months and take up space, getting dusty. We've learned to order the minimum, test the product, and restock if it sells well."

"You are wise beyond your years, Annie." She motioned to the first hallway. "I'm this way."

"Did anything specific catch your eye?"

"Everything. That's the problem, but I'll heed your wisdom and place small orders. The other thing that has shocked me is how wonderful the authors have been. They're gracious, and most of them have said they'd be thrilled to come to the store for a signing. Maybe they're being kind to an old woman." She started to take a sip of the tea but decided against it as the totes slipped down her arm.

"I doubt it. It's a win-win. Authors can meet their readers in person, and you get more foot traffic in the store. Again, I would caution you to plan for smaller gatherings. We learned that the hard way at the Secret Bookcase. There's nothing worse than setting up the Ballroom for a hundred people and having three show up."

"That would ruin me." Laurel set her teacup on the floor

and dug through her tote bags in search of her room key. She grabbed her reading glasses on the chain around her neck and positioned them on the tip of her nose to get a better look. "I would feel terrible for the author."

"Yeah, it's not fun. That's what prompted us to start thinking bigger with things like the Mystery Fest and our holiday gingerbread competition."

"I should hire you to do my marketing. You're a treasure trove of good ideas." She finally found the key and buzzed us into the room. As she picked up her tea, the cup slipped and spilled liquid down the front of her sweater. "Oh dear. Oh no. Look at me. I'm a mess."

"You didn't burn yourself, did you?" I asked with concern.

"No, this is lukewarm at best. Would you mind putting the books on the table by the patio doors? I'll go change."

"Do you want me to wait?" I asked.

"I was hoping to pick your brain if you have a few minutes?" She patted her chest as if hoping to dry the tea stain magically.

"I have time. I'm going to the mystery panel, but that won't start for a while."

"Oh, lovely. I'll be back in a flash." She disappeared into the bathroom.

I took her books to the table as promised. Her room was a mirror of mine, only on the opposite side of the pool. She had a patio with two chairs, a potted palm, and views of the grounds and cabanas.

I considered opening the slider and sitting outside to wait for her. The sparkling sunshine on the shimmery blue pool was tempting, but something else caught my eye. A device. A headset. Not any headset. *The* Headset. Fox Andrews's Headset rested on her bedside table.

I crept closer to get a better look.

My pulse raced.

A prickly feeling spread down my neck.

Yep, this is it.

This is the Headset.

It was undeniably the Headset. Fox's logo was branded on the band, but what was even worse was the instruction manual sitting next to the VR headset. Someone—most likely Laurel— had scribbled notes and scratched out certain sections in the manual.

I scanned the room for anything I could use to pick it up. I didn't want to touch it. Laurel's fingerprints would be all over the Headset and manual, and if she had engineered it to kill Fox, I could be looking at a prototype of the murder weapon.

THIRTEEN

"Sorry it's taking me so long. I'm having zipper issues," Laurel called from the bathroom. "I'll be right out."

"Take your time," I replied, hoping she would do just that.

Think, Annie.

I had limited options and a short amount of time. I couldn't risk Laurel seeing me with the Headset or manual. I couldn't take it, but if I left it, she could get rid of the evidence before I had a chance to speak with Detective Greene.

My only play was to take photos and text her immediately.

I snapped pics of the Headset and opened the manual pages. Then I found a tissue in my purse and used it to turn the pages and take more pictures carefully so as not to touch any part of it with my fingers.

I heard the bathroom door opening.

Shoot.

I pretended to sneeze, "accidentally" dropping the tissue on the floor.

"Are you okay?" Laurel came around the corner wearing a new pair of slacks and another thin cardigan. She'd changed out her glasses chain to match the outfit.

"Allergies," I lied, picking up the tissue and bunching it in my fist. "Whatever is blooming has been irritating my airway."

"It's that time of year. I suffer terribly from a drippy nose. I believe I packed over-the-counter allergy medication." She pointed to the bathroom. "Would you like me to check?"

"No, that will just put me to sleep." I stuffed the tissue into my bag. "I'll be fine."

"Okay, shall we secure good seats for the mystery panel, then? I don't want to keep you." Was it my imagination, or were her eyes lasered on the Headset?

Did she realize I'd seen it?

She plastered on a smile and wiggled her earlobe. "I don't hear very well, so I prefer to sit near the front."

If she suspected I had seen the Headset, she gave no indication. She babbled on about in-store events as we made our way to the panel. I was desperate to text Detective Greene, but with Laurel as my shadow, that was going to prove challenging.

She stood at the top of the stairs and pointed with a quivering finger to a couple of empty seats in the second row. "Oh, look, there. Those are perfect."

This was my chance. I had to relay the information to Detective Greene before Laurel returned to the room.

"I might go grab a coffee. I didn't sleep well last night. If you want to hold me a seat, that would be great, but if it fills in, don't sweat it."

"Consider it done." Laurel nodded with a purpose. "Will your friend, Fletcher, is that right, be joining us?"

"He said he was going to try to attend, but his girlfriend just arrived in town, so I'm not sure. You don't need to worry about him." It wasn't that I didn't want to save Fletcher a seat, but I wanted to get away from Laurel and fill Detective Greene in immediately. This was a big break. It couldn't wait.

"I'll see what I can do." She used the railing to descend the stairs, keeping a tight grip on her book totes as she made her way toward the front of the auditorium.

I hurried to the lobby, texted Detective Greene the pictures, and briefly explained what I'd seen. Then I poured myself a cup of coffee I didn't need; my body already felt like it was twitching with possibilities.

Could Laurel be a killer?

She had a strong motive that she hadn't been shy about sharing—Fox had used her store for his own financial gain without her permission (at least technically speaking). Was the sweet, little old lady vibe an act?

Questions swirled through my mind as I added a splash of cream to my coffee.

She'd mentioned that her grandson was a tech wiz.

Maybe my initial take on how she could have done it was correct.

Or what if she had a background in technology? Her husband, Albert, could have been an engineer or developer, or for all I knew, she worked in the industry.

Detective Greene responded immediately:

> Thank you. Where is she now? Still in her room?

> Theater—second row.

> On it.

I put a lid on my coffee and fell into step with Fletcher and Victoria, who were leaving the showroom.

"Excellent timing," Fletcher said, gesturing to Victoria like introducing royalty. "Annie, you remember Victoria."

I punched him in the shoulder. "Yeah, I saw her two weeks ago at the store." I rolled my eyes and leaned in to hug Victoria. "It's great to see you, or should I say, be formally introduced?"

She tilted her head to the ceiling and chuckled. "I like to tease him that he's my formal Fletcher." Victoria was as tall and thin as Fletcher. She wore her hair in a tight bun and was dressed in a halter-top sundress that hit her high above her knees. "You look wonderful, as always, Annie. Full of color and energy."

"Thanks." I smiled, touching my cheeks, which were warm. "The color could be due to what just happened."

"That sounds ominous," Fletcher said with a frown.

"I helped Laurel take some things to her room. I'll spare you the details, but long story short, she spilled tea and had to change. You're never going to believe what I found."

"Now I'm really intrigued." Victoria rubbed her hands together softly. "This feels like we're in a murder mystery."

"We are, and I might have found tangible evidence that Laurel is the killer."

"Laurel?" Fletcher sounded confused. "She's low on my radar. I'm still cued in on Theodore."

"Maybe they're working together because look at this." I stopped to show them the pictures I'd taken on my phone.

"That's Fox's Headset." Fletcher zoomed in like he couldn't believe what he was seeing. "How did Laurel get it?"

I tapped the screen. "Look at this. She also has a user's manual with all sorts of notes and things crossed out."

"I've seen things like this on *CSI*," Victoria said, peering over Fletcher's shoulder. "It's like instructions for building a bomb."

"Yeah, a bomb that was detonated in the middle of yesterday's panel." I shuddered at the memory.

Victoria reached toward me, placing her manicured hand on my arm. "I'm so sorry, Annie. I shouldn't be making light of the situation. You've been through a horrid ordeal."

"It's fine," I assured her. "Trust me, one of the coping strategies detectives use when working a serious case is finding moments of levity. It *does* feel like a *CSI* script. I just can't quite understand how Laurel pulled it off. She doesn't seem like she has the technical savvy, but then again, she could be deliberately giving that impression."

"A partner makes the most logical sense." Fletcher handed me my phone. "Did you tell Detective Greene? Have you seen her lately?"

"I texted her right before I saw you two. I think she's on her way to the theater to find Laurel now."

"What are we waiting for?" Fletcher grabbed Victoria's arm. "Let's go watch the fireworks."

The fireworks were subdued. When we took our seats, Detective Greene was ushering a very confused Laurel out of the auditorium. Laurel caught my eye and shrugged as if she had no idea why the police were calling her away. I wondered if Detective Greene would be successful in gaining access to Laurel's room. She needed a warrant unless Laurel invited her in willingly.

It was nearly impossible to concentrate on the panel. The writers were witty and engaging, but my thoughts kept returning to Laurel. Could she have pulled off Fox's murder? I didn't want to be ageist, but she didn't strike me as someone well-versed in VR devices. Selfishly, I also liked her. Her story about opening the Last Chapter after her husband's death had moved me, but I couldn't let my personal feelings cloud my professional judgment.

I barely realized the panel was over until the audience broke out in applause. I caught myself and joined in, clapping and rising to my feet.

Detective Greene was waiting for me outside of the theater. Like yesterday, she was dressed professionally yet casually in a pair of capris, sandals, and a floral blouse. "Thanks for the intel."

"Did she confess?" I asked hopefully. That would make for

an easy case and free me up to fully concentrate on my next steps with Silicon Summit Partners.

"No." Detective Greene shook her head. "We took her in for further questioning."

"What did she say about the Headset?"

"Here's the kicker. She let me into her room."

"Really?"

Detective Greene pressed her lips together as she nodded, almost like she wished it weren't true. "She claims a box was sent to her store last week with the Headset, a gift from Fox's publicity team for the use of her store."

"A 'gift,' that's rich." I used air quotes to emphasize "gift." "After what he did to her—exploiting her store for his own financial gain." Laurel must have been fuming when she received it, which only made more questions bombard my brain —like why did she bring it with her to the convention?

"Her sentiments, too." Detective Greene shrugged. "I don't know if I buy her story."

"What about the manual? If the Headset was a gift, why did she mark the instruction book?"

"Apparently, her grandson used it. She wasn't interested in it, so she passed it on to him. He made notes about glitches and little issues with it. She brought it along to give to Fox. At least, that's what she's saying for the time being. We'll see if she sings a different tune at the station. A couple of hours in a cold, windowless room might prompt her to tell the truth."

"Do you think it could be her prototype? A practice Headset?" I wracked my brain for other possibilities.

"I sent both to our tech department, so we'll have to wait and see what they come back with. Nothing seemed off in my preliminary examination of the device, but I wasn't about to try it on the off chance it's rigged, too."

"Smart."

Her phone buzzed. She opened it and checked it quickly. "I'll let you know what I hear."

"I appreciate it." I was pleased she was willing to keep me in the loop. "While I have you, Fletcher heard a very different story from Theodore at breakfast this morning."

"Really? I'd love to hear more." She took out her notebook and waited for me to proceed.

"His story changed dramatically. He used a connection on the board to secure his spot as the moderator, and according to Fletcher, he said it was intentional because he wanted to confront Fox."

"One sec." She held up a finger and flipped through her notes. "That's what I thought. Theodore's official statement matches what he told you. Looks like I'll be speaking with him again next."

"It also sounds like he may have more technological expertise than he originally let on."

"Noted." She closed the notebook. "I don't know whether we'll release Laurel, but you should prepare for her to approach you if we do. She asked if you had alerted me to the Headset being in her room. I didn't divulge any details, but—"

"But she's smart and can easily put two and two together." I finished her thought. "Don't worry. I assumed as much, and I firmly stand my ground on the issue—this is a murder investigation. I can handle her."

"I don't doubt it." Detective Greene nodded in agreement, readjusting her ponytail.

I was tempted to ask her if she knew anything about Silicon Summit Partners. The company was in her jurisdiction. She could have dealt with them before, but bringing another person in on my plan at this stage was risky, especially someone in law enforcement.

"You've got my number. Text or call if you stumble upon any further evidence. Watch your back while you're at it."

"I will." I wasn't concerned about a confrontation with Laurel, but the more questions I asked and the more Fletcher and I dug into the suspects' pasts and connections to Fox, the harder it would be to fly under the radar. Odds were good that the killer would realize what we were up to, which meant we needed to proceed with caution.

FOURTEEN

I texted Pri and Liam to see how the coffee tasting was going:

> Are you buzzing yet?

Pri replied first:

> One word—chococcino!!!

> Is that code?

Liam answered for me:

> It's her new obsession.

> Dense hot chocolate with whole milk and vanilla. Caffeine-free—aka I can have as many as I want. Don't tell Penny. I'm in love.

Pri added chocolate bars, hearts, and drooling emojis to her message.

I was glad they were pacing themselves on the caffeine intake. I let them know that Operation Silicon Summit was still on and that I'd check in again once I was on campus. I studied the schedule to see what I wanted to attend next.

Victor Moore was slotted to demo his Read Moore on the pool deck. Perfect. That would give me a chance to see the tech in person and hopefully chat with him about Fox. I was curious how Fox gained access to Victor's e-reader and if he'd copied it to the letter or taken parts of it to use in his Headset design.

The crowd was smaller than I anticipated, although Serena was signing in the vendor showroom, so that might explain the lackluster turnout. When I passed by on my way to the pool, the line was already wrapped to the door.

Victor hastily set e-readers on the two tables he'd pushed together. "Give me a moment, folks. I'm running behind. Got held up with this police business, but I'll be ready to start in just one minute." He was dressed in another Read Moore T-shirt, a pair of shorts, and flip-flops. He could pass as one of the many surfers who ventured into Redwood Grove after a day of riding the waves.

"Held up on police business" sounded like code for Detective Greene had interrogated him again.

I stood with the rest of the group, watching Victor wrestle with the e-reader setup, his face dripping with sweat. It didn't seem like a particularly taxing task, and the temperature outside was balmy, with a nice breeze wafting over us, making the palm leaves dance. His damp hands fumbled with the devices, leaving smudges on the screens. He kept pausing to grab a towel and wipe his forehead and the e-readers, muttering under his breath like he was cursing his nerves. People grew increasingly impatient.

"Do you need help, man?" a guy near me asked.

"No. I've got it. I was just caught off guard. Take a beat. Give me a minute. Apologies. I didn't realize it was so hot out here. I would have asked for a room inside with air conditioning, but I think we've got it." He flung the towel around his neck like a boxer cooling off between rounds. "Go ahead, come closer. Don't be shy. This is a hands-on demo. You're free to pick up the Read Moore and take it for a test drive."

"What's the concept behind the reader?" a bookseller I'd met earlier asked.

"I'm glad you asked. She's my audience plant, everyone." He attempted to crack a joke. It didn't land. A few people forced awkward chuckles. "Yes, the concept. Right. Uh, what exactly are you asking?"

The bookseller caught my eye. She looked as perplexed as I felt. "According to the blurb in the convention brochure, you're touting the Read Moore as a revolutionary new e-reader, but what's revolutionary about it?"

Victor yanked the towel off his neck and dabbed his forehead like he was trying to dam up a flood of incoming sweat. "Okay, yeah. Let's get into it." He tossed the towel on the table and picked up one of the e-readers. "You all are booksellers, correct?"

Nearly everyone nodded.

"This is going to be a game changer. I guarantee the Read Moore will be your bestseller this year."

"But what is it?" someone interjected.

My question exactly.

Victor rolled his shoulders like he was getting into character. Then he massaged the screen gently and launched into a full-scale pitch. "We're talking hyper-personalized recommendations. By analyzing readers' gaze patterns, the Read Moore determines what captivates the most attention—genres, themes, even writing styles. Then it uses that data to suggest similar books." His body language shifted as he gained confidence. "It uses real-time engagement metrics. It's measuring what parts of a book hold readers' attention the longest. It identifies cliffhangers, emotional highs, or parts where the story slows and gets bogged down. We're sharing that data with authors and publishers, too. Imagine how this kind of information and feedback is going to shape the future of reading. We can literally show an author the exact sentence where the reader dropped off and closed the book for good."

"I'm not clear how this is an advantage to bookstores?" the bookseller asked.

"This is just the tip of the iceberg." Victor set the e-reader down, speaking with his hands as he became more animated. "We have adaptive reading features built in. The device adjusts font size, brightness, and layout based on the reader's eye strain and focus level, creating the optimal reading experience. It will automatically highlight and save passages the reader's eyes linger on. For readers with dyslexia, it uses gaze tracking to assist with voice-to-text narration and adjusts the reading speed."

I was pleasantly surprised to hear how much thought had gone into accessibility features for the e-reader. That area was often overlooked or an afterthought, but it was clear that access for all readers was a priority for him. We were committed to making sure every reader had an enjoyable experience at the Secret Bookcase. Our shelves and displays were spaced far enough apart to accommodate wheelchairs, and the Terrace had a ramp for anyone with mobility issues. We stocked a variety of large print and audiobooks and held a monthly signed author event with an ASL interpreter.

But at the same time, I was overwhelmed by the pace of all the new technology being featured at the convention. Sure, it was great to see the book world evolving, but truth be told, at the end of a long day, all I wanted was the comfort of curling up on the couch with a well-loved paperback and Professor Plum on my lap.

"Our AI, combined with eye-tracking movements, can also infer emotional responses to content and make recommendations based on how the reader feels. So, for example, it might suggest an uplifting romance, gripping thriller, or relaxing cozy, depending on the reader's mood. That's where you come in as booksellers. The Read Moore constantly tracks preferences across multiple genres, continuously updating a curated TBR. We're integrating that TBR with bookstores, making it seamless for readers to access new books." He paused to catch his breath. "We're exploring so many possibilities. The Read Moore can instantly suggest books on sale at your store that match the reader's preferences. It can also track underappreciated books that line up with the reader's niche interests. This is great for helping lesser-known authors gain visibility and for those of you who carry used books in your stores."

I had to admit, his pitch was good. Like my fellow booksellers, I'd assumed the Read Moore was just another e-reader.

"Please, come give it a try. I think you'll be blown away by what this beauty can do." He motioned to the table.

People queued for their turn with the Read Moore. I waited to speak with Victor. He answered dozens of questions about the logistics of linking the e-reader to bookstores and the retail price point. Everything he shared about the product did indeed sound like it could transform the reading experience and also the broader publishing and writing ecosystem, but I couldn't pick up a thread or connection with Fox's Headset unless Fox had stolen and incorporated the eye-tracking sales data. Laurel had mentioned the Headset could order books directly. Maybe that was the piece he'd copied.

By the time Victor was free, the crowd had dissipated.

"Annie, right? We met yesterday at the panel where, well, you know..." He didn't finish his thought before extending a firm hand. "What did you think of the Read Moore? Did you have a chance to try it?"

"It's impressive, especially the accessibility features." I already had a few loyal readers in mind who would appreciate those benefits.

"Thanks. That's important to me. My sister is dyslexic. She's my inspiration for the Read Moore. She loves to read now, and she's my beta tester for any new updates." He reached for one of the devices. "I didn't have time to get into the latest additions, but we're working on an interactive storytelling element."

My senses perked up. Storytelling elements sounded more in line with Fox's Headset.

"We're still in testing phases, so this won't roll out onto the market for a while, but the idea—and this also came from my sister—is to create interactive books that adapt their narrative based on where the reader's eye lingers. Think of it as a modern take on a choose-your-own-adventure novel but without overt choices. We're working to hire authors to write multiple plot points. The story would change and unfold naturally based on the reader's subconscious interest."

"Wow. That's huge." I could imagine the concept being a big hit with our younger readers, but I still found myself internally cheerleading for the faded yellow pages of a physical book. There was nothing quite as romantic as flipping through pages that dozens of other hands had touched over the years, wondering if the same passages had moved another reader.

"Right? Yeah." He bounced from one foot to the other. "It's cutting-edge stuff. Reading will look entirely different in the next decade."

I wasn't sure how I felt about that, but this wasn't the time to engage in a philosophical discussion.

"It sounds similar in some ways to what Fox was trying to achieve with the Headset."

His head jerked as his body tensed. "Why would you say that?"

"The interactive and immersive storytelling. They definitely have some crossover, don't you think?"

He gave me a piercing stare, crossing his arms tightly over his thin body. He took a slow, deliberate breath as if trying to compose himself before responding. "No, the only crossover between our products is what Fox snatched from me."

There was my confirmation.

Victor struggled to contain his reaction to my question. His body quivered, a red flush spread up his neck, and his fists tightened into two balls. I wondered if he hadn't been able to contain his anger at Fox and employed a plan to see that Fox could never steal from him again.

FIFTEEN

"Fox stole your technology—did he use it in the Headset?" I could hear my voice rising in surprise.

"He tried, but I saw through him immediately." Victor's tone was clipped, like he was trying to hold it together and avoid an outburst.

"I've heard this from several people. It seems to be a pattern."

"That's an understatement. He came to my headquarters, which at the time was my mom's garage. Thanks to venture capital and the incredible enthusiasm surrounding the Read Moore, we've moved into our own offices."

"Congratulations. That's a big step."

"Yeah, the expenses keep piling up. I was excited to be out of the garage, but now, in hindsight, free rent wasn't so bad." He reached under the table, grabbed a box of antiseptic wipes, and started cleaning the e-readers.

I laughed and tried to steer the conversation back to Fox. "It must have been a while ago that you and Fox met."

"The early stages of prototyping." Victor averted his eyes and scrubbed the screen. "Fox caught wind of what we were doing from a mutual friend. He already landed a bunch of VC money. I should have been smart and had him sign an NDA, but I was starstruck. The name 'Fox Andrews' is synonymous with success. I thought he was interested in investing."

"He wasn't?" I asked, already guessing the answer.

"Not then, no. He wanted a demo. We geeked out together —engineer to engineer. I thought he was genuinely interested in the Read Moore. I was naïve. I showed him everything, even our back-end algorithms and AI prompts. He told me I was going to be the next Steve Jobs, you know, starting my company in my mom's garage; then he proceeded to plagiarize every- thing I'd worked years to create and try to pass it off as his own."

That aligned with Laurel's and Theodore's experience with Fox. If nothing else, Fox Andrews had been a skilled scammer, finding the right loopholes and tactics to get his victims to give him what he wanted.

"What happened after that?" I pressed, hoping to keep him talking.

"Turns out Fox wasn't a great coder." Victor laughed, but there was no warmth in his tone. "He couldn't replicate my code, even though I let him take notes and pictures like an idiot. I guess that's karma. That's why the Headset is so shoddy. It's a terrible product because Fox was a terrible engineer. He had an original idea; I'll grant him that, but his execution was awful. He lost a chunk of his venture capital. If he were smart, he would have hired a professional engineer or a team with the investment money, but he tried to do it all himself, and it blew up on him."

I felt my body tense at his word choice.

He must have noticed because he shook his head. "Sorry. I didn't mean it like that."

"It's okay. I understand you must have been upset."

"Upset. Ha!" He tossed the wipe in a garbage can nearby

and grabbed another. "Try fuming. I was ready to burn his house down."

Again, his phrasing didn't leave anything to the imagination.

"Who does that and thinks they can get away with it?" Victor picked up another tablet and stared at it like a new mother fawning over her baby. "I worked for five years. Five years on the Read Moore. I missed out on friends and dating and the things you're supposed to do in your early twenties because I was singularly focused on this." He cleaned the screen more gently this time. "It's fine. You have to make sacrifices for your dreams, but then to have Fox come along and try to rip it all right out from under me. Nope. No chance I was letting that happen."

"What did you do?" I was half-expecting him to confess to murder.

"I hired a lawyer. What else could I do?" He shrugged. "That failed, too, but then, in a twist of fate, Fox came crawling back to me."

"Crawling back to you?" One of the tricks I'd learned in my criminology training was mirroring a suspect's words back to them. It was deceptively simple yet remarkably effective—encouraging them to elaborate, clarify, or even slip up as they heard their thoughts reflected.

"Can you believe it? Fox Andrews showed up at my new office begging me, on his knees, begging me to partner with him. He couldn't get the Headset to perform. The reviews were terrible. Readers hated the product. It was a fail—a complete bomb. He was about to lose the last of his VC cash. It was sweet justice to watch him beg for my help. Not to mention, it was pretty brazen of him. He stole my algorithms, AI prompts, and code and then came groveling back."

"I'm confused about the partnership piece. Did Fox want to hire you to fix the Headset's issues?"

"You and me both. He wanted to partner. He claimed that one of his venture capitalists was very interested in the Read Moore. He proposed a joint partnership where we would merge both companies and launch the e-reader and the Headset simultaneously."

"What did you say?" My brain raced to make connections. Fox had approached *him*. That was a new twist.

"What do you think?" He raised his eyebrows. "Look, I won't repeat what I said because it's not appropriate. Let's just say it involved telling him where he could stick something."

"Did you consider it even briefly? Would it have helped your launch to have Fox's money?" It was still challenging to comprehend the rapid transformation Victor, Fox, and their counterparts were pushing when it came to the book industry. I didn't want to close myself off to the changing technologies, but none of these devices could replace the magic that lived within the walls of the Secret Bookcase, at least in my opinion.

"He didn't have money. He had nothing. I saw right through him the second time. You know the saying—fool me once, shame on you. Fool me twice, shame on me. There was nothing Fox could have said to entice me. No amount of money would be worth going into business with him. I don't want my name associated with him or his worthless product. I told him in no uncertain terms to leave and showed him the door." He stacked the clean tablets in a pile.

"How did he react?"

"He wouldn't take no for an answer. God, that guy. Talk about the ultimate narcissist. What story did he tell himself? He was still trying to convince me yesterday. I told him desperation was a bad look. He claimed to have tweaked the Headset and hired a kid to fix the coding. He wanted me to demo it. I refused. I didn't owe him anything. And, as you saw, the Headset is rubbish."

"Although the police suspect someone tampered with the

Headset," I said. I didn't think Detective Greene would mind. Word had spread, and Victor had been so forthcoming.

"I heard that, but I doubt it's true. The thing sparked like fireworks when he brought his 'new and improved' version to my office. I wouldn't put that thing anywhere near my body, let alone on my head. The guy had plenty of enemies, so I guess it's possible, but it probably malfunctioned like all his other product fails." He gathered the e-readers. "I should go. I have another panel. Let me know if you have other questions about the Read Moore. I'd be happy to pay a visit to your store and do a demonstration for your entire staff."

I watched him grab the tablets and scurry inside.

I didn't blame Victor for turning Fox down. I wouldn't want to work with someone like Fox either, but nothing I'd learned thus far absolved him of murder. Sure, Fox begging for his help with his defunct Headset made me inclined to think Victor wasn't the killer, but his animosity and resentment were palpable. There was a very real possibility that Victor wanted him ruined in every way. He'd admitted his coding skills were superior to Fox's, and he'd had access to the Headset. Could he have exacted his final revenge by using Fox's Headset against him?

SIXTEEN

"So what did you think of the Read Moore?" A guy fell into step with me. I turned to see Phillip Kaufman hurrying to keep pace with me. I hadn't noticed him at the demo. His tailored black suit and black-rimmed glasses would have stood out amongst the T-shirts and shorts that most other attendees wore.

"Were you at the demonstration?" I motioned behind us to the pool with my thumb.

"No. I was meeting with a potential client. I can't divulge any details—it's still too early in the process. We're waiting for the ink to dry on the contracts, but trust me, it's a huge win for Cloudbound." The eager glint in his eye and the way he lingered over "huge win" practically begged me to ask more.

"It sounds like congratulations are in order."

"Uh, no, it's not a done deal yet. I don't want to get ahead of myself. I've been burned before. I guess you don't need the gory details, do you?" He stopped in mid-stride like he realized he'd said too much. "I'm cautiously optimistic," he said, continuing forward. "But I've been in this business long enough to know that you never pop the champagne until the contract is signed. I've lost out on several books I loved and thought were mine at the last minute. The only thing that's different this time around is that I don't have an editorial board to convince. It's just me. I live or die alone by the authors I sign."

"How has it been striking out on your own?" I asked, scanning the lobby to see if there was a spot we could sit. I had questions for Phillip, and this was the perfect opportunity. Two couches opened up near the coffee and tea station. "Do you want to sit for a minute?"

"Certainly." Phillip paused to pour himself a coffee before joining me. He started to take a drink but decided against it, resting his cup on the wicker coffee table before sitting down. He took off his suit jacket and hung it over his arm. "You asked about starting my own publishing empire."

"Empire, huh? I like that." I grinned. "You're not thinking small."

"You can't think small in this industry. Publishing isn't for the faint of heart. I lost one of the bestselling series of all time at auction during my first year on the job after an editor at a different house used less-than-ethical tactics to pile on extra bonuses and perks under the table for the author. I learned then you have to do whatever it takes to get ahead."

My senses perked up. Did doing "whatever it takes to get ahead" involve murder?

"We hear the end result of auctions on the bookselling side," I said to him. "If a book has gone into bidding wars, that's always included in the marketing and publicity materials. Seeing how publishing houses position those books and reader responses is always fascinating. Sometimes, titles with tons of buzz don't resonate with readers, and sometimes, they become bestsellers. You must have a good sense that a book will be successful before going to auction."

"Definitely. You need that passion." He carefully placed his folded jacket on the arm of the couch and launched into a lecture on how the process worked. "Auctions aren't the everyday norm, but they're the dream—at least for authors and agents, not for me. I can't tell you how many sleepless nights and tense days I've had when I can clearly see a book's originality and commercial potential, but I know eight other editors are standing in my way."

Again, his choice of words was noteworthy—"standing in his way" and "doing whatever it takes to get ahead." I let him continue but made a mental list.

"Once an agent recognizes bidding war potential, it's an all-out battle." He clenched his free hand into a fist. "We call it the bloodbath before the book deal."

"I've always wondered, is it a straight-up auction, where the highest bid wins?" Again, maybe it was just semantics with a phrase like "all-out battle," but in my world, words mattered.

"It depends on the agent. It can be the best bid where editors submit their highest offer upfront. Agents will also offer round-by-round bidding. I've seen multiple rounds for proven authors. And sometimes there's a preemptive offer, where a publishing house tries to bypass the bidding process by offering a significantly higher deal to lock down the manuscript."

"That sounds stressful," I said truthfully, feeling my skin turn hot at the thought. My stomach twisted imagining how intense it must be to be caught up in that kind of chaos. Thank goodness I worked in a cozy bookshop where the biggest stressors of our days were tracking down mis-shelved titles or debating whether to rearrange the staff picks display in the Foyer for the third time in a week.

"It is," he admitted, exhaling sharply. "It's dramatic. Often more dramatic than what's on the page." His fingers tensed into a fist briefly before he forced them to relax. "Losing out on a hot manuscript stings. It also can be a blow to your career. Winning a bestseller can elevate your status in a house. That's why it sucks when editors come in with extra incentives like film options, foreign rights deals, or a guaranteed release schedule, especially if you have a firm budget. That's the pro of being on my own. I can swing for the fences."

"But that must mean pressure, too. You need the book to return on its investment, right?"

He crossed his legs and leaned back on the couch like he was settling in and getting comfortable. That was a good sign. I wanted to keep him talking about publishing and subtly segue the conversation to Fox's murder. Building trust with a suspect was key. The more relaxed he became, the more likely he would let something slip.

"True, but I'm investing in myself at this stage of my career. I know books. I know what sells. I can spot a standout manuscript and future bestseller in the first three chapters. Now I'm not tethered to a corporate agenda or budget. It's scary, but it's entirely freeing. Signing this new client is going to have a ripple effect in the book world, and I can't wait." He paused and knocked on the coffee table. "Knock on wood, that is, but I have a good feeling after our discussion this morning. I explained to them that I have flexibility and the ability to be nimble and pivot in ways that the Big Five can't. They're behemoths. My clients get the best of both worlds: an editor with a stellar track record of breaking out authors and building long-term careers with a fresh perspective on where the market is headed."

This was my chance to steer the conversation toward Fox. "You mentioned that briefly on the panel. Are you considering adding features like virtual reality into contracts? Speaking of fences, I'm still not sure about some of the technology. I love a good old-fashioned book in my hands."

"That's fair. But you have to be forward-thinking. That's where big publishing fails. They're stuck in the dark ages. They won't even entertain most of the new digital products and technology featured at the convention. It's only been within the last few years that they've moved away from written editorial feedback on printed manuscripts." He muttered something under his breath I couldn't quite make out.

"Were you partnering with Fox to offer that to your clients and future clients?"

"Do you know about Fox's history?" He squinted and studied me like he was trying to read my response.

"I'm not sure what you mean. His work history?" I noticed a band setting up near the bar and hotel staff members blowing up polka-dot beach balls. It must be for the party later. I was sad to miss out on the celebratory bash, but Scarlet's murder and getting face time with Logan were my priorities. Time was running out and I needed to get on with my mission while I had the chance.

"His history in *publishing*," Phillip said pointedly.

"No. I had no idea he had a connection with publishing."

"Oh yeah, a big one. He put my last publishing house out of business."

"What? How?" I was tempted to break out my notebook or phone so I could transcribe our conversation for Detective Greene, but I didn't want to do anything that might put Phillip on the defensive. My memory would have to suffice.

"As I mentioned, I spent nearly fifteen years at one of the big houses. When I left, I bumped around a little. I was with three other midsized publishers with varying degrees of satisfaction."

I didn't want him to go on a tangent about his personal work history, but I didn't want to cut him off, either, so I nodded, encouraging him to continue.

"The smaller and midsized houses have limited budgets and resources. There were no extensive marketing campaigns or high-profile promotions that the big houses could afford. That meant many promising books I worked on underperformed and never lived up to their potential because they had insufficient exposure and support. I strategized with my authors on grass-roots marketing, but watching books never find a readership was frustrating. Good books—books that very well could have hit the *NYT* list with the marketing machine of a big house behind them."

"I get that." I smiled at a staff member carting huge inflatable floaties in the shape of popsicles and ice cream cones to the pool. "We're inundated at the bookstore with advanced reader copies and promotional materials. I hate to say it, but it's easier for us to order larger quantities of a new title from a reputable and known publishing house."

"That's the rub. The other challenge for me was wearing multiple hats. In addition to juggling my editorial duties, I acted as a marketing coach and liaison, acquisition scout, and even had to manage production timelines. The burnout rate was high. I struggled to maintain the level of attention to detail that I expected and wanted to provide for my authors."

"How did Fox become involved? Did he pitch a virtual reality assistant?"

"I wish." Phillip scowled and shook his head. "No, this was before he invented the Headset. He was a junior editor and a slick talker. He convinced the editorial director to take a chance on an algorithm he created that supposedly would be able to track sales, manage delivery deadlines, automatically upload digital files, and much more. How he convinced them his app would work, let alone invest in it, is beyond me. It ultimately ended up bankrupting the company because none of his promises worked. It was a total failure. Every employee was laid off without severance pay because they'd spent so much trying to fix the bugs in Fox's technology there was no money left."

"That must have been terrible for you."

"Terrible for me. Eh. Maybe." He shrugged. "Although, in some ways, it was a blessing in disguise. I'd been wanting to strike out on my own, and not having a job forced the issue. It was worse for my authors. The company is still embattled in a legal nightmare because they stopped paying royalties. They owe authors hundreds of thousands of dollars."

"How recent was this?"

"About a year and a half ago. Fox came out of the bankruptcy unscathed. He took the money he got from the company and invested it in the Headset. That's how he was able to build it—on the backs of editors and authors. Ironic, isn't it?"

Ironic. Yes. And a motive for Phillip to want Fox dead? Possibly.

SEVENTEEN

"I'm so sorry, that's awful," I said to Phillip. "Did you keep in touch with Fox, or were you surprised to see him on the panel?"

"Oh, no. I've been watching him since he brought down the publishing house. I've kept up on his endeavors and tried to warn people, not that anyone will listen."

"I got the impression on the panel you were interested in the Headset and other technology that could enhance your authors' writing and marketing efforts."

"I am. That's true." He picked up his coffee and took a sip before making a face and setting it back on the table. "I didn't realize we'd been talking so long. My coffee has gone cold." His phone dinged with a text. "Will you excuse me? One of my authors."

"Of course. Thanks for the information on book auctions. I'll have so much more insider information to share with readers. I have a feeling it might make some readers even more inclined to give a book with a lot of buzz a try."

He left with his cold coffee. I took a minute to gather my thoughts and take quick notes to share with Detective Greene. I wasn't sure what to make of Phillip's perspective. We'd gotten cut off before I could learn exactly how he intended to use technology like the Headset for his clients. He played off getting let go without severance mildly like it wasn't the end of the world. Maybe he had a nest egg or money saved away from his previous publishing career, but he couldn't have been pleased about being out of work. However, I couldn't argue with the idea that sometimes a loss turns out to be the catalyst for great change. If it hadn't been for Scarlet's death, I wouldn't be pursuing my dream of running Novel Detectives or being a partial owner of the most fabulous bookstore on the planet. The same could be true for Phillip. Maybe being laid off really had been a blessing in disguise.

The other piece of information I wanted to pass on to Detective Greene was Fox's failed publishing algorithm. It was yet another example of his engineering failings. The more I learned about him, the more I was convinced he was a great salesperson, perhaps even a visionary, but he obviously lacked the skills to see his ideas through to fruition.

Phillip, Victor, Serena, Laurel, and Theodore each had a motive for killing Fox. I wanted to hear from Detective Greene whether they'd gotten any more information out of Laurel. While her being in possession of the Headset kept her on my list, I still wasn't convinced she had the technical savvy to pull it off. The outlier could be that she'd enlisted the help of her grandson; that seemed dark, though. Everything about her persona was open and welcoming. Just the fact that she was finally pursuing a lifelong dream of owning a bookstore made her less likely to have killed him in my eyes. And leaving the evidence in plain sight in her hotel room? Why would she invite me in if she knew there was a decent chance I'd see the Headset?

Victor and Theodore both remained high on my list. Theodore had lied about moderating the panel and seemed to have a vendetta against Fox, and so did Victor. Even though Fox had come crawling to Victor for help, it didn't erase the seething fury Victor felt over Fox's betrayal. The audacity of Fox's request only fueled Victor's fire.

I also had more questions about Serena's history with Fox. Had he sent her a test version that malfunctioned to the point it caused a migraine? She was militant about protecting her sources and clients' anonymity. Understandably so. If she believed Fox was planning to solicit her highly curated clientele, that gave her an undeniable motive.

The morning had vanished.

It was already lunchtime. That meant it was time.

Oh God.

It's time.

My throat swelled. My ears felt like they were on fire.

I swallowed hard, forcing the fear not to bubble up, and sent a group text to Liam, Fletcher, and Pri:

> On my way to SSP. Wish me luck.

My phone lit up like a disco ball.

> Be safe, Annie!

Pri sent three fingers-crossed emojis.

Liam's message seconded the sentiment.

> Trust your gut. Don't push it. And get the hell out of there if anything feels off.

He closed out his text with a kissing and strong-arm emoji, making me slightly less stressed. Liam thought I could do this. I knew he had my back no matter what, and his advice was solid. If things went south, I wasn't taking any chances.

A final text dinged on my phone.

Standing by. Waiting for my orders

Fletcher added, signing off with a spy emoji.

I freshened up in the bathroom, mainly to buy a minute to center myself with a pep talk. Hal always told us never to undervalue the influence of positive words. I pictured him and Dr. Caldwell cheering me on as I checked my reflection in the mirror.

You've got this.

You've trained. Prepared. Planned.

My cheeks were bright with color, probably due to the nerves tumbling in my stomach.

Annie Murray, you are a kick-ass private investigator—a criminologist. You have justice on your side. Now, go get it.

I almost gave myself a fist bump but figured it would be just my luck that someone would walk in. I gave my appearance one last check, grabbed Fletcher's Risk Analysis packet, and headed outside.

The warmth of the afternoon brought a natural spring to my step. Or maybe that was the fear and excitement pulsing through every cell in my body. I took the route we'd walked to the restaurant last night, repeating a positive mantra. Everything smelled fresh like summer had settled in for good. Kids laughed and shouted as they darted through front yards and biked in happy gangs to the community pool with towels and goggles tossed over their shoulders. Somewhere down the street, the nostalgic jingle of an ice cream truck brought a rush of summer memories—Scarlet and I lounging on the quad. Me with a paperback and her with her notebook, drawing elaborate mazes and character sketches of everyone passing by. We'd soak up the sun until my freckles started to pop and then head to the HUB for ice cream sandwiches. Scarlet would show me her intricate drawings. She loved hiding Easter eggs in her sketches and timing me to see how long it would take me to find them.

Oh my God—that's it!

Her sketches. Her Easter eggs.

On a whim, I'd packed her old journals and brought them with me to the hotel. As soon as I was back in my room, I wanted to give them another look. What if she'd hidden the answer there? It would have been just like her to hide a clue for me in plain sight.

I could almost feel her laughing at me, tapping her watch, and saying something like, *It took you long enough, Annie.*

Overhead, the palm trees swayed lazily, arching above me like they were whispering a quiet prayer for my safe passage. I needed it because Silicon Summit Partners loomed in front of me like a heavily guarded fortress. The main entrance to the investment firm sat down a long, intimidating gated driveway that seemed designed to deter all but the most determined visitors. A heavy, black gate stood as a formidable barrier. Two security guards patrolled each side of the gate. Their severe uniforms and no-nonsense stance gave me a moment of pause.

My breath caught in my chest.

You can do this.

I took another step forward.

"Can I help you, miss?" the first guard asked, his hand going straight to the Taser secured to his waist. His ballistic vest and combat boots made him look like he was protecting the White House, not an investment firm.

"I have a meeting." I tapped the file tucked under my arm and pointed to the driveway lined with trim hedges, hoping my confidence would be enough to let me through. In the distance, the glass-fronted building glinted in the sunlight reflecting the heat.

"Sign in here." He thrust a clipboard with a pen attached at me.

I wrote my full name, the date, and the time and handed it back to him.

He scanned the sign-in sheet like a proctor administering an exam. Then he tapped a line next to my name. "You missed this section. How long do you intend to stay?"

"Sorry. I didn't fill it out because I'm not sure." I gave him an eager, impish grin, playing up my naïve, bookish act. "It's an interview. Do you know how long they usually last?"

"If you're lucky, an hour." He wrote my anticipated exit time on the sheet and buzzed me in.

"Hopefully, I'll get the job. Wish me luck." I crossed my fingers.

Okay, step one. Success.

I took a long breath for courage as I marched down the driveway and arrived at the twenty-foot glass doors. The lobby reminded me of a swanky hotel. Gleaming marble floors looked like they'd been newly polished. Plush, modern furniture was arranged in clusters, accented by minimalistic coffee tables and artful floral displays. A soft hum of instrumental music played in the background. A bank of elevators to my left was my ticket to Logan's office, but they were blocked by a long reception desk.

"Welcome to Silicon Summit Partners. Are you meeting with one of our investment bankers?" The receptionist greeted me with a forced smile and a once-over.

I could tell she was judging my attire. Since I wasn't wearing designer clothes or expensive shoes, I figured she wouldn't peg me as one of their high-profile clients.

"Yes," I returned a wide smile.

"Oh." She masked her surprise and clicked her computer screen.

"Who are you meeting with?"

"Logan Ashford."

She blinked and snapped her head to the side. "Logan Ashford?"

"Yes, that's correct."

She typed on her keyboard, frowning and running her finger along her screen like she was double-checking she wasn't missing something. "Logan doesn't have any client meetings on his calendar today. Are you sure you're here at the right time?"

"Positive."

"What did you say your name was?"

"I didn't. It's Annie Murray."

She checked again, her posture becoming more defensive. "You're not on his schedule, Annie. I can't help you. I can give you his card and you can call or email to make an appointment with him or one of our other bankers."

"He'll see me."

"What?" Her nostrils flared. "What do you mean?"

"Call him and tell him I'm here." I nodded to her phone and wrapped the file folder to my chest, standing my ground. "He'll see me."

"Do you have a personal connection with Mr. Logan?" Her lip curled as she assessed me.

I had to give her credit for doing her job. She wasn't going to let me in without a fight.

"Yes." I smiled widely but didn't elaborate.

She huffed and appraised me again, trying to decide if she would be in more trouble if she did or didn't call him. My unassuming bookseller outfit, complete with my purple glasses, must have done the trick because she picked up the phone, keeping a steely on eye on me like she was worried I might race her to the elevators.

"Mr. Ashford, sorry to bother you. There's an Annie Murray here to see you. She doesn't have an appointment, but said you know her?" Her voice was filled with trepidation.

I almost felt sorry for her, but she worked for the enemy. Whether she knew it or not, I was doing her a favor.

"Yes, Annie Murray." She nodded, holding my gaze with a look of utter distrust. "Uh-huh. Yes. That's correct."

My heartbeat thudded so fast it felt like a jet trying to take off in my chest.

Please let this work.

Please let this work.

"Okay." She shrugged and hung up the phone. "He said you can head up. Third floor. The office at the end of the hall."

This was it.

Time to confront Scarlet's killer.

EIGHTEEN

My body vibrated and hummed like an electric current on the short elevator ride to the third floor. Ten years, countless tears, nights spent poring through old police files, and scouring Scarlet's college notebooks had led to this—this very moment.

Despite the throbbing in my chest and the tingly feeling spreading up my arms, I wasn't afraid for myself. I was... What was the word I was looking for?

Ready.

Yeah, ready.

I inhaled deeply through my nose and then slowly released my breath.

I am ready.

I stepped off the elevator, sucked in another gulp of air, squared my shoulders, and marched down the long hallway to Logan's office, keeping the fake documents tightly tucked under my arm.

My footsteps echoed in the corridor where the marble in the lobby continued. The floors had been polished and scrubbed to the point I could almost skate on them. A hint of a strong antiseptic cleaner hung in the air, mingled with the distinct scent of corruption.

The space was the antithesis of the warm and cozy vibes of the Secret Bookcase. It was sterile and soulless. Glass office doors gave the appearance of openness, but there was barely a whisper or brush of movement despite the fact that every office was occupied by Logan's minions. Staff sat in their fishbowls, their faces backlit by blue computer screens. No one so much as bothered to look away from their laptops as I passed by.

That was fine with me.

I wasn't here to network.

I was here for Logan Ashford.

Logan Ashford.

His name was etched on the glass door at the end of the hallway.

I pretended to hesitate. I had a role to play.

"Mr. Ashford." I knocked timidly on the door. "It's Annie Murray."

"Yeah. Enter." Logan motioned me in with two fingers like he was summoning a servant.

His desk was designed to intimidate. It was constructed out of black marble. He hid behind it, not bothering to stand to greet me. A picture of the bookseller dressed like Dorothy from *The Wizard of Oz* flashed through me. That was Logan Ashford in a nutshell: the wizard, a shell of a man, a fake, a phony. I knew from my research that he loomed large behind the desk because he wasn't much taller than me. I studied enough photos of him to notice he wore lifts to appear taller and was always photographed with his employees or clients strategically positioned around him, seated at his desk like a king.

His dark hair was slicked with gel in a way that made it look crunchy and damp at the same time. I couldn't tell if he spent hours by his private pool, tanning in the sun, or if his bronzed skin had been sprayed to achieve its leathery look.

"Sit," he commanded, using an expensive pen to point toward the skeletal black chair with a spindly frame resembling a gaunt horse. A bizarre choice of furniture—or art? Another sign that he went out of his way to ensure anyone who entered his office felt uncomfortable and out of place.

He clicked the pen twice and studied me with a mocking curl of his lips. "You're here to play detective. How cute. Is this your Nancy Drew look? You're missing a magnifying glass."

I wanted to reach across the desk and strangle him, but I had to maintain my composure if I was going to pull this off. "No, actually the opposite." I placed the documents Fletcher had prepared in my lap.

He hadn't expected that response. I could tell from how he stiffened ever so briefly and clicked the pen rapidly again as if trying to readjust his expectations. "I'm unclear what the opposite of that might be. Please, enlighten me, Ms. Murray."

"I'm guessing you're aware that I met with Mark."

"Mark?" He leaned back against his chair and swiveled from side to side. I half expected him to prop his feet on the desk and break out a cigar.

"Mark Vincent, your former employee?" I asked innocently. I knew the game we were playing, and I intended to win.

"Look, kid, I have hundreds of employees. I'm the CEO of a Fortune 500 company; do you think I know every staff member's name?"

Logan was hitting all the right nerves. I hated being called "kid." I wanted to correct him but had to stick to my script. "Mark filled me in on Scarlet and her contract with you. That's why I'm here. I need a job." I wrang my hands together, pretending like I was anxious and desperate. I didn't mention anything about Mark trying to run me off the road or Elspeth, the fake psychic Logan sent to Redwood Grove to try and threaten me. When Fletcher and I had brainstormed our options for getting into the building and finding the evidence

Natalie had stashed, we decided the best path was to ignore all of that and lean into desperation. We needed him to believe that Natalie had toed the company line and not divulged any of her secrets.

I'd rehearsed my lines. I knew what to say next.

There was no doubt that Logan was floored by my statement.

He froze in place, his hand mid-motion to click the pen. Then he stopped abruptly as his eyes widened, and he blinked rapidly like he was trying to process if he'd misheard me.

It took every bit of resolve not to give him a haughty smile.

His lips parted slightly as if he was going to speak, but no words came out.

I took that as my sign to launch into my pitch. "I won't lie. I know you're aware I've been trying to find Scarlet's killer."

"News to me." He set the pen on the desk and tapped his computer screen. "It's not as if I haven't been inundated with your emails, requests for private employee records, and blatant accusations. I thought you had some nerve showing up here. Now you're asking for a job. This is going to be rich."

"I admit I got it wrong, okay?" I hoped my tone sounded appropriately humbled. I'd practiced my dog-with-a-tail-between-its-legs routine with Liam at least a dozen times. "I believed Silicon Summit Partners was responsible for Natalie's death. When Scarlet and I were assigned her case as our final senior project, we came to the conclusion that someone within the firm must be responsible for her death, whether it was an affair gone wrong or—"

He cut me off. "Or an employee trading insider secrets. If Natalie hadn't disappeared, she'd be in prison right now."

So that's how he's spinning it.

Good to know—interesting.

I can work with that.

"Natalie was involved in insider trading?" I asked, widening my eyes and tapping my foot on the floor.

"That didn't come up in your *research*?" The way he enunciated "research" didn't leave room for doubt. He was dismissing me. This was exactly where I wanted him. "Talk about nerve. I gave her a start. I helped her build wealth and taught her the ropes, and how does she reward me? By stealing company intel and using it for her benefit. Insider trading is a federal offense. She should be behind bars."

"Do you have any idea where she is?"

"Probably on a beach on the Cayman Islands sipping a mai tai with my money." He tossed his head back with a sinister laugh.

"I had no idea. That makes so much more sense. I can't believe what I missed." I pounded my forehead with my palm. "But I think you have bigger problems than that."

He carefully set the pen in its case and folded his hands together. The gaudy gold rings on his hands seemed more like weapons for his knuckles than a fashion statement. "I'll give you a break since you were a college kid when this started, but it's been ten years. It's time to let it go."

"That's exactly what I'm trying to do. That's why I'm here." I gestured with my hands, sitting up taller and becoming more animated. "After I met Mark, I realized that I'd made plenty of leaps when it came to Scarlet. My professor cautioned us about jumping to conclusions, but I couldn't separate myself from the case. Scarlet was my best friend. She had her entire life in front of her—so much potential and so many dreams cut short." I tapped into those raw feelings, the disbelief and grief of the first days after we learned she'd been killed. My eyes misted. I brushed away a tear.

Logan ran his hand along his jawline. "She was a sweet girl. She would have done well here. We were excited about bringing her on."

"That's the thing. I never knew she was applying, interviewing, or even in discussions about working for you. I guess that's the reason I was so clued into Silicon Summit Partners, but then, when I met Mark, my entire theory fell apart. He told me she had signed an employment contract and was planning to start working with you. I still can't believe it." I dabbed my eyes with my fist, hoping to keep selling my emotional reaction to being in the building and talking to him. He was a hard guy to read. I felt like he was buying it, but he wasn't unintelligent. For all I knew, he was seeing right through me.

"She kept it secret because she signed an NDA as part of her employment. She couldn't tell you. It would have negated her contract. That's how business works, kid."

"Oh my God, why didn't I think about that?" I placed my hand on my chest and let my mouth hang open in surprise. "Of course. Did you ever reach out to her family after she died?"

"Why would I do that?"

"I just wondered if that was standard practice." I ran my finger along my chin. "It must have come as a shock to you to learn she had been killed. Can I ask—she was going to be assigned to your internal affairs team, is that right?"

He looked bored with the conversation. "We have robust internal affairs, investigation, and security teams that protect our assets, our clients, and our reputation. Scarlet was going to be in a blended role, working with our risk management department, fraud investigators, compliance officers, and cybersecurity. She wasn't clear on a specific direction for her career, so I suggested a crossover role for her first year. We do that for stand-out new hires. We have rigorous training programs. By floating between teams, we can analyze employees' skill sets and the best position for promotions and determine whether they're candidates for long-term roles. This isn't an easy place to work; many of our new hires only last a few months. If you make it to the year mark, you're here for life."

For life? That sounded ominous.

"Is that how Natalie came up through the company?"

A tiny but noticeable flash of irritation crossed his face. "As I've already stated, Natalie abused my trust and her position at the company."

I needed to steer away from asking more about Natalie. "I take it you were impressed with Scarlet during her interview?"

He nodded. "She knew her stuff. She was professional, especially for a recent college grad."

I wanted to interject that because of him, she technically never graduated.

"She would have done well here. I had high hopes. It's a shame they never were able to find her killer."

If he was trying to bait me into a reaction, I wasn't going to bite.

I blinked away false tears and considered my next move. Logan was a chess master. I felt like I was in a battle with him, but in this instance, my next move could be my last if I wasn't careful.

NINETEEN

"Tell me more about why you want to work for Silicon Summit Partners," Logan asked, his tone leery.

This is where I really have to bring it.

I could easily lose him if I don't play this right.

I sighed heavily for effect and then launched into my script. "Honestly, part of it is selfish. My world was rocked when Mark explained that Scarlet intended to work for you. I haven't been in the field for the last ten years. I've been working at a book-store in Redwood Grove. Scarlet's death left me scattered. Don't get me wrong, I've loved being a bookseller, but this past year, even before meeting Mark, I've been feeling like it's time to take a different path. I've been assisting the local police with a few investigations, and I just took and passed the state exam for private detectives, with flying colors, I might add. I can show you my certification." I reached for my bag on the floor.

"No, that's not necessary. What's the selfish part?" He dismissed my attempt to provide him with my credentials with a flick of his fingers.

"Scarlet." I took a second to pretend to compose myself. "I don't know if she mentioned this during her interview, but we were planning to open our own private investigation firm after college. I guess that's one of the reasons it hit so hard to hear that she had already signed an employment contract with you."

He stared at me like he was running out of patience and ready for me to get to the point.

"Because of Scarlet, I've reignited my passion for this field of work, and I guess it feels like it would be coming full circle to work for you, a way to honor Scarlet."

He was about to interrupt, but I held my index finger to stop him and handed him the folder. "Sorry, I just have to say I'm not expecting a handout or special treatment. I know I'm good. I have a breadth of experience I didn't have when I was first out of college—life experience, people experience. My track record for solving cases is high, as in one hundred percent. I'm analytical and exacting when it comes to an investigation, and I also operate from my intuition. I have excellent references. I just need a chance. I need a shot. I want you to take a look at that document."

He massaged the back of his neck and frowned. "I appreciate the passion, but we began this conversation with the fact that you were wrong about me and my company. That isn't exactly a stellar pitch of your skills."

I couldn't believe how accurate our conversation was playing out compared to the practice runs I'd done with Fletcher, Liam, and Pri. This was verbatim what we'd sketched out. I didn't wait for him to respond because I knew he wasn't going to entertain my quest much longer. "Take a look. These are the cases I've solved in the last year, along with an in-depth risk analysis of Silicon Summit Partners. Many of your methods are outdated. What happened with Natalie is the tip of the iceberg. You're in real danger. You have a mole in the firm, leaking company secrets. It's only a matter of time before the press catches wind of these major gaps in your internal security. Once they do, it will be a firestorm for you. I can find the mole if you'll give me a chance."

He leafed through the twenty-five-page document Fletcher and I had prepared. Fletcher deserved more credit than me. He had forgone sleep and showers. Hal and I teased that he should have considered a career path working as a special investigator for the CIA or FBI.

"I discovered some serious flaws in your physical security." I played the video I'd shot of the guards letting me past the gates with my simple lie on my phone while he continued to scan the documents. That had been Pri's suggestion. "Your receptionist, too. If there's an entry policy for visitors, it should be non-negotiable. I slipped past your first two lines of defense with a small lie. That alone should worry you, but your issues are much, much bigger. One of your employees is linking intel—insider trading—that comes with nasty penalties and jail time, and it's obviously been happening for years. I think Scarlet realized it, and now I'm ready to finish what she started."

He pinched his fingers to zoom in on my phone screen.

Do I have him?

Is this actually working?

My foot bounced faster on the floor. I pressed my hand on my thigh to force my body not to betray me. Not now.

"Okay. I'm listening." He rested the folder on the desk, handed me my phone, and held my gaze. "What exactly are you proposing?"

"You give me the same opportunity as Scarlet. Except I don't want to start as a novice, though. You're holding proof of what I can do. Let me meet with your teams and start digging. There's a mole, and someone like me on the outside is perfectly poised to find them. We can start on a trial basis."

His beady eyes darted from me to the door and back to me again. "What kind of a trial?"

"Um, maybe three months?" I glanced at the calendar on his

desk like I was checking it for reference. "I'll need time to get a better lay of the land and to interview staff. You can hire me the same way the police do—as a consultant, and then we can revisit our contract at the end of three months. If we're both satisfied, we can renegotiate."

He eyed me with a sharp, scrutinizing gaze. The kind that seemed to peel back layers.

I felt entirely exposed.

The silence stretched out as if he was daring me to say more.

But then he let out a sharp laugh, throwing back his head. There was no warmth in it—just cold amusement. "Damn. You really had me with the glasses and the whole librarian act. But you make a fair point. I'll give you one month." His words were deliberate, carrying a threat he didn't have to say out loud and his eyes lingered on me a bit too long, like he was reminding me silently who was really in charge.

"One month?" I sighed, biting the side of my check deliberately as I pretended to consider his counteroffer. "I don't know if that's enough time to make inroads."

"You want a chance? One month." He folded his arms across his chest to show that was his final offer.

"Okay, it's better than nothing." I bobbed my head and tapped my fingertips together. "Can I start now?"

"Now? As in today?" His voice dropped to a menacing calm.

"Yes. I need immediate access if I only have a month. I'm only here for a short amount of time with the conference. I'd prefer we keep this between us. You can tell your staff I'm on special assignment for you or working on my grad school dissertation, but it's important they don't suspect I'll be observing them. That will come in the next phase."

"Next phase?"

"I need to return to Redwood Grove and work out an

arrangement with my current employer. I can commute in the short term. I think it's better if I'm only around for chunks of time. It's fewer opportunities for employees to wonder what I'm doing."

The conflict on his face made me almost giddy.

"We haven't discussed your rate."

I made a little circle with my finger, pointing to Fletcher's handiwork. "If you flip to the last page in the document, you'll find my rate along with my references and my initial plan of action."

He had no answer for that. "Uh, all right. Why don't you head down to the lobby? Get a cup of coffee. I need to speak with HR and put together a contract."

"I'll also need a key card with full access."

"Not going to happen." He shook his head, leaving no room for negotiation. "We have an extensive vetting process for our security team. Only a handful of employees have key cards that allow them to enter most rooms, but no one other than me has full access."

I anticipated he would say that. "Fine, but I need a green light to enter the building and access to HR."

"HR?"

"Employee records. That's the first stage of my inquiry."

He looked like he wanted to do anything other than grant me this request, but he motioned to the door. "I'll see what I can do."

I wanted to sprint down the hall, but I measured my steps.

Jackpot!

I was in.

I'd actually done it!

Logan might think he had the upper hand, but he had no idea what was coming.

TWENTY

The receptionist gave me a cold stare when I returned to the lobby. "You can sit over there." She motioned dismissively to the collection of couches.

I texted the group:

> Phase one complete!

> Did he bite?

Pri sent another round of fingers-crossed emojis.

> Yes. I mean, don't think he bought it. He's not an idiot. But he's talking to HR about a contract. I'm cautiously optimistic. More soon.

> Cool, cool. We're stopping by Serena's signing. Will keep you posted if we learn anything from her.

I couldn't blow my cover by showing too much excitement, so I picked up a magazine from the collection on the coffee table and pretended to be captivated by a story about a wild horse sanctuary in Southern California. In fairness, the article was interesting, but my heart was still pounding from my meeting and my mind was swarming with possibilities. Concentrating on the remainder of the day was going to be nearly impossible. I was already counting down the hours until nightfall when I could return with a key in hand, buzz through the gate, and find the evidence Scarlet had oh-so-wisely stashed.

"Annie Murray?" A woman stepped into the lobby, summoning me like I was being called into the principal's office. Although she reminded me more of a prison warden with her dull gray suit and pointed heels.

"That's me." I stood and raised my hand, a reflex left over from my school days.

"This way." Her heels clicked on the marble floor.

I hurried to catch up to her.

She pressed the call button on the elevator and kept her back turned away from me. Our ride to the second floor was silent. "Follow me," she said, again without so much as a glance, and then proceeded to power-walk down the hall.

Her office was nondescript, with state-mandated HR posters framed on the walls and a neatly organized desk. "I'll need your driver's license and social security number." She pushed a stack of papers at me. "Fill these out. Be sure to sign or initial everywhere that I've flagged."

I handed her my license and took the forms. "Have you worked for Silicon Summit Partners for a long time?" I asked, hoping to make small talk while I filled out the mountain of paperwork.

"Logan explained what you're doing. I'm not participating in this nonsense."

"Nonsense?" I played it off like I was shocked by her response. I removed my glasses and set them next to the stack of paperwork.

She ignored me and typed my information into her

computer. It was like I was being given the silent treatment. What exactly had Logan said? And where had he gone?

I didn't like this. He agreed to keep my role under wraps, but if he'd already told HR about our arrangement, was that a sign that he was going to track my movements?

I needed to proceed with caution. That was true regardless, but I couldn't assume Logan didn't have a trick or two up his sleeve—or worse, a plan to take me out like he'd done with Scarlet.

After I completed and signed the paperwork, the HR director thrust a welcome packet across the desk. "Review this. It contains everything you need, along with a copy of your contract."

"What about a badge and a key? Also, will I have an assigned desk, or will I float when I'm in the building?" I kept my tone bright and upbeat.

"It's in the packet. Read it." She pointed to the office next door. "My staff will take your picture for your badge. Anything else?"

I had about a million other things I would have loved to ask her, but her tone made it clear our conversation was finished. "No, thanks." I left with a wide smile.

It didn't take long to get my badge and key card. Soon, I was walking back to the hotel with an employment contract and a way to get back into the building. I could hardly believe my plan worked—or at least had worked enough to gain me temporary access.

The rush of adrenaline buzzed through me, sharpening my senses. Everything outside seemed bright; the sun blazed overhead. Every color popped—the deep greens of the manicured hedges, the flash of a white car breezing by, the electric blue of the sky. Every sound was crisp and clear, from the chirping of the birds in the trees to the buzz of the security gate shutting behind me.

Even my own breathing sounded louder in my ears.

I allowed myself a minute to savor this, to take it in, knowing this brief victory wouldn't last. I was in for now, but this was just the first step.

Fletcher was pacing in front of the hotel when I returned. "Annie, I've been channeling my inner Holmes, but you're going up against your own version of Moriarty, which is making it difficult to remain calm." He captured me in a hug.

Big shows of affection weren't his style.

I squeezed him back. "It went almost exactly as we scripted. I've got a key." I dangled my badge.

"How was he?" He winced in anticipation like he already knew what I would say.

"Gross. Condescending. Everything we thought and even worse. He never got up from his desk. I'm convinced it's because he didn't want me to see how short he is. Spoiler alert— I already know."

"Does the key get you in the front door?" Fletcher asked. "What about the rest of the building?"

"I specifically asked for building access, but that was a no. I had to go with plan B. I could tell that he didn't trust me. Your documents sealed the deal, but he's on high alert for sure. I left a little something behind. I think it's the best, well—only—way in." I tapped the folder with the Silicon Summit Partners logo embossed on the front. "Now that I'm a legit contractor, I only need to get past the guards. I should be able to put together a sob story about forgetting my favorite pair of glasses in my excitement to sign the contract. We'll be dealing with the night crew anyway. They don't interact with most of the staff, so I'm not worried about that part."

"The oops-I-forgot-my-glasses plan." Fletcher pretended to search our surroundings for an imaginary pair of frames. "That means I'm on surveillance. I might need to cancel the meetup. But that's fine—uh. Wait, what part are you worried about?"

"It's not clear how the security system is set up. Will Logan get notified if I show up later tonight, even if the guards clear me? And what's his level of distrust? Did I sell the story well enough that he won't be on the lookout for something like this from me tonight? I mean, obviously, he doesn't trust me, but to what degree?" I pulled out the badge. "Is this tagged? Will he get alerted immediately? Or is he assuming—like we hope—that I'm planning to dig around for the next few weeks, and he can keep an eye on me while he crafts a plan of what to do next?"

"What does your gut say?" Fletcher ran his finger along his jawline, considering the implications of my litany of questions and bringing me back to center almost immediately.

What does my gut say?

"I'm not sure." I exhaled slowly, tucking the badge back in my bag. "He went along with it, but that could mean he's planning his own stakeout tonight, and I show up to a trap."

"That's why one of us should come with you." Fletcher frowned and hardened his gaze. "It's not smart to go in solo, especially in the middle of the night. This is the one major flaw in plan B."

"It's the only option. The guards aren't going to let me in with someone tagging along."

Fletcher massaged his angular jawline, deep in thought. I knew not to interrupt him when his eyes glazed over like this. After a minute, he snapped and held up his finger. "Got it! What if you play it up like you and Liam were on a date, had too much wine, and realized you had misplaced your glasses? You can stumble in and pretend like you're tipsy and need your glasses desperately. Even if they make Liam wait outside, at least he'll be nearby if things go south."

"Maybe." Having Liam on the premises didn't sound like a bad idea.

"Well, you're not going to like this, but I've already

suggested Liam should find a way to tag along with you, and needless to say, that *is* the plan. I've been poring over my Sherlockian knowledge trying to figure out how to get both of you inside, and that's it. You can play drunk, right? Watson has done much worse at Sherlock's bidding. And I cannot begin to relay the various disguises and techniques Sherlock has used in his quests to capture killers. Drunk Annie is our play."

"Uh, I... guess—"

"There's no guessing. I'm putting my foot down, Annie Murray." He stomped to prove his point. "I've considered this long and hard. There's a reason Watson always accompanies Sherlock. Backup, my dear Annie. Backup. You can't do this alone. Liam is in full agreement. I've been toying with a variety of options for him, including posing as one of the members of the evening custodial crew, but all of them require him to have access as well. Accompanying his drunk girlfriend is a much simpler sell."

"Okay, but you didn't even know what the next plan would be. We talked through so many options."

Fletcher raised his eyebrows knowingly. "Come on, Watson, you didn't actually believe Logan Ashford would give you carte blanche, did you?"

I sighed and adjusted the new-hire packet under my arm. "No, but a girl can dream, right?"

He wrapped his arm around me in a brotherly fashion. "Always, but until you have hard evidence in your hands, let's keep you securely grounded in reality. Remember, we made a deal, no unnecessary risks."

"You're right." I leaned into him, returning the hug. "I know. I'm excited because it feels like this might finally happen, but I don't trust Logan, and I don't want to underestimate him. I'll work on my drunk act this afternoon."

"Excellent." Fletcher saluted. "Now, on to other news.

Laurel was released. She's asking for you. I told her you were on an errand, but I'm sure she'll seek you out, so consider this your warning."

"Detective Greene must not have had enough to hold her. I wonder if that means she cleared our sweet bookseller or if she needs more evidence to make an arrest."

Fletcher shrugged. "Your guess is as good as mine. I haven't seen Detective Greene for the last hour or so."

"How are things with Victoria, and are you still planning on attending Victor's meetup later?"

"It's wonderful to be reunited with her," he said with a blush blooming on his thin cheeks. "I should bring Victoria along with me. Victor and Victoria has a nice ring to it."

"Wasn't that a movie?"

"Oh, Annie, we do need to keep you abreast of culture, don't we? It was a musical, in fact, starring the one and only Dame Julie Andrews. If memory serves, I believe it debuted in 1983."

I put my hands on my hips and raised an eyebrow. "So ten years before I was born. Were you even born then?"

He gave me a crooked, mischievous smile. "Wouldn't you like to know?"

"I would. You're not that much older than me. Six or seven years? I don't think you were born in 1983."

"Maybe I was. Maybe I wasn't." He held his hands palms up, tilting them back and forth like unbalanced scales.

I rolled my eyes. "I need to put this in my room, grab another pair of glasses, and check in with my pet sitter. See you later?"

"Count on it. Pri and Liam will be here promptly at five. They gave me strict instructions to ensure you are poolside and ready to recap. Understood?"

"Understood." I nodded seriously and headed for my room.

I couldn't wait to see them both and fill them in on my meeting with Logan. We had much to discuss and the next phase of our covert operation to plan. Plus, any distraction between now and my return to Silicon Summit Partners would be welcome.

TWENTY-ONE

I didn't have to seek out extra distractions because Laurel accosted me at the entrance to the book hall after I returned with a new pair of tortoiseshell glasses. "Annie, dear, oh, good. I've been searching everywhere for you. I feel terrible about what happened earlier and want to explain myself." She still had her assortment of mismatched totes, but the distinct dark powder on her fingers told me Detective Greene had required fingerprints.

She didn't appear to be angry with me for betraying her secret.

"Could we walk and talk?" She gestured to the festive strings of twinkle lights and colorful bunting stretched between the booths. "I've just returned from the police station, and I'm concerned I gave you quite a scare. Please let me apologize." She gulped, batting her eyes like she was struggling to fight off tears and dipping her head toward the floor.

I considered it for a minute before responding. Laurel seemed genuinely apologetic and sincere. Her openness made me more inclined to be honest with her and I wanted to hear her side of the story. "I wouldn't say a scare, but finding the

Headset and instruction manual in your room was a shock," I said, proceeding into the colorful showroom. It was like a feast for my book loving senses. Delicious scents of garden mint and strawberry book candles, aptly named Book Crush, greeted us at the first booth. I paused to smell one and made a note to come by later to get a better look.

"I understand, and I don't blame you in the slightest for alerting the police. I would have done the same thing in your shoes. They even took my fingerprints like I'm a criminal. Me? A criminal." She held out her hands to show me as we continued past booths featuring book phone cases, reading lights, and elegant stationery. "I should have mentioned it to you. It completely slipped my mind. I did notice you seemed in a hurry to get a cup of coffee, but then again, far be it from me to stand between anyone and their caffeine." The lines etched on her forehead deepened as she smiled. "I can only imagine what you must think of me. I explained this to the police, but let me put you at ease: That was not the Headset that killed Fox."

I never thought it was, but I didn't say that to her.

"You see, Fox sent me an early prototype as a thank-you for allowing him to shoot footage of the store. Never mind that I had no idea of his intended usage, but that's aside from the point. I didn't want the monstrosity. What would I do with a virtual reality headset? I think I may have mentioned my grandson is a technical wiz. He was visiting, and the Headset caught his eye immediately. I gave it to him and didn't give it another thought until he called me and began rattling off all sorts of glitches and issues with the device."

"What kind of issues?" I asked. The Headset malfunctioning was the key to the investigation. If I could only figure out *how* the killer had tampered with the Headset, then I might be able to solve the case.

"Strange buzzing sounds. Odd vibrations. Shaky video quality. The list goes on and on. He's a smart kid, and that's not me being a biased grandma. He's top in his class with a four-point grade average. He's on track to graduate early and has already received interest from some prestigious universities. I suppose I sound like a proud grandmother, don't I?"

"Rightfully so. Your grandson is obviously a great student." I paused again, a display of book maps catching my eye. Fletcher was a book-map connoisseur. If he'd stumbled upon the vendor, it was a sure thing that he'd already put in an order for every map from Green Gables to St. Mary Mead.

"He's been tinkering with electronics since he began to crawl," Laurel said proudly, pulling my attention away from the captivating maps.

I assumed she was speaking figuratively. I couldn't imagine many parents offering their toddlers electronics to "tinker" with.

"By the time he was in third grade, he was taking apart computers and rebuilding them. His dad is in the industry, so he comes by it naturally. We tease that he inherited those genes from his father's side of the family. My daughter is bookish and a reader like me. We love hearing about his projects, but honestly, he's light-years ahead of either of us."

"Which is why you gave him the Headset?" I tried to imagine doing something similar when I was his age. In my awkward teen years, I preferred to get lost in a book. Not much had changed. Reading was still always my preferred pastime.

"Yes. He was over the moon to try it, but his hopes were dashed when he realized the many flaws in its design. Those are his notes you saw in the manual. He called me to ask whether I could put him in touch with the inventor. I'm sure it sounds silly to an outsider, but he thought he could help make the Headset better or at least marketable. He told me none of his friends would spend any of their holiday or birthday money on the device. He couldn't use it for more than a few minutes without getting sick."

Serena Highbourn had mentioned the same thing. "Did it give him a headache?"

"Yes." Her mouth hung open, and her eyes widened in shock. "How did you know? The headache was so bad it made him sick."

"I've heard that from a few other people who beta-tested the prototype." We managed to walk by a booth of book totes without her taking a second look—a small miracle. She was clearly too wrapped up in trying to explain herself that her focus was entirely elsewhere.

"These kids play games online for hours." She gestured with her hand like she didn't approve. "My grandson said no one would buy the Headset as is. He believes it needs a complete overhaul. Oh, I can't recall the technical terms he used, but he tore it apart and came up with new pathways and algorithms. I think that's the right word. That's why I brought the manual with me. My grandson marked up the manual with his suggestions for fixing the device. I noticed Fox was on several panels, and I wanted to pass on my grandson's feedback."

"Wouldn't that help Fox improve his technology? I was under the impression you were furious with him."

"I was. I am." She rubbed her fingers together, almost like a reminder that she'd been accused of his murder. "That didn't change, but I would do anything for my grandson. It would be a big boost to his college applications to be able to list that he'd been instrumental in perfecting a product and that his suggestions might be implemented."

I didn't respond right away. I felt like there was more she wasn't saying.

She picked up a set of colored pencils that were being given away at one of the booths and grew quiet.

After we moved on to the next booth, she drank in a breath like she was trying to work up the courage to speak. "The truth is, I figured Fox owed me. He hadn't asked for permission to use my store in his virtual reality headset, so I intended to force a favor and have him hire my grandson. I'm not proud of that. I realize it sounds like blackmail. I'm sure that's what the police think. I wasn't planning to ask him for money, but I was going to suggest that my grandson would be a good addition to his team. I didn't have any power over him. I couldn't technically force him to do anything, but it was worth a shot. It's so challenging for kids to get an 'in' these days. Since Fox owed me for filming at the Last Chapter, he could make it up to me by hiring my grandson or at least giving him an internship."

"Were you able to speak to him about your grandson's suggestions?" I was glad I had listened to my intuition and waited. This was exactly the kind of revelation I was hoping for. Laurel attempted to strong-arm Fox into hiring her grandson as payback. What else was she capable of?

"No. I was waiting for the right opportunity. I intended to speak with him after the panel, but then he died before I had a chance."

"Thanks for being honest with me."

"I'm sorry I didn't mention it sooner. I feel terrible that you found the Headset and where your head must have gone. I'm surprised you didn't call 911 or make a citizen's arrest on the spot."

I ignored that. I didn't want to get into the specifics of what making a citizen's arrest entailed. "What did the police say?"

"The usual. They told me not to venture out of the area and that they would likely be in touch with further questions."

"And you explained all of this to them?" I was tempted by the warm, buttery aroma wafting from a nearby bakery booth, where intricately decorated book-themed cakes and cookies were displayed like edible works of art. Fondant bookmarks peeked from layers of luscious sponge cakes and frosted cookies mimicked the covers of classic novels.

"No, thank you." Laurel kindly dismissed the baker, offering us samples of chocolate, lemon, vanilla bean, and raspberry cake. She nodded to me, motioning toward the exit. "Shall we head out?" Without waiting for my reply, she moved on, sinking back into her story. "Yes. I didn't have much of a choice. They asked if I wanted a lawyer. I hope I didn't make a mistake by declining, but I don't have anything to hide. Everything I've told you and them is true. My family will back up my story. They know the entire saga with Fox. Well, I suppose I failed to mention that I was planning to strongly encourage Fox to hire my grandson, but they'll tell you that he had the prototype and all the glitches he found. I gave the police their contact information. I hope they speak with my daughter and son-in-law. It's so stressful to go through an ordeal like this without my husband. He would have known exactly what to do."

I was inclined to believe her and was suddenly craving a taste of the raspberry cake with lemon buttercream, but we were nearly back where we started, and I could tell our little chat was coming to an end.

Her story checked out and matched the consensus that the Headset was nowhere near ready for the market.

The fact that Detective Greene had released her also made me think she likely believed Laurel's story.

But until Fox's killer had been formally arrested, I couldn't remove her from my suspect list. There was still a chance she was desperate for revenge and to give her grandson a leg up in the competitive college application process.

Was there a possibility she could have enlisted his help without him understanding the ramifications?

Or was she telling the truth?

Was she a kind bookseller, pursuing a dream and eager to see the next generations of her family pursue their dreams, too?

TWENTY-TWO

"I've been talking your ear off. I'm sorry. We did a full lap of the convention hall with me blabbing on and on like I tend to do." She glanced toward the exit. "Here I go again, chatting about me and my problems. I seem to be doing that often. I just had to get this off my chest." Laurel looked at me like she was trying to decide whether I was angry with her.

"I appreciate you sharing. It's helpful," I said honestly.

"I would hate to think that you don't trust me now. You are a kindred spirit and have been so generous in sharing your knowledge and ideas. This entire convention is overwhelming, and you're a bright spot." Her eyes misted.

If she was lying, her acting skills were superior, and I didn't think they were. Her need to explain herself and clear up any misunderstanding made me more inclined to believe her.

"I'm glad you told me the truth and that you spoke with the police. The only thing that matters to me is finding Fox's killer."

"Me too." She pressed her hands together in a show of gratitude, momentarily forgetting about the fingerprint ink. "Oh dear, I'm a sticky mess. I won't take any more of your time. I need to go wash up. Enjoy the evening."

I watched her shuffle into the crowd. Selfishly, I hoped it wasn't her, but until Detective Greene made a formal arrest, I intended to keep my eye on Laurel.

The convention was in full swing. Booksellers chatted happily in cozy nooks in the open lounges and poolside cabanas. People mingled as they hurried from one panel to the next, while others took their time meeting with vendors and placing orders for the holiday season.

I was at a crossroads. I could attend one of the afternoon panels and try to take my mind off Logan and Silicon Summit Partners until Pri and Liam returned from their coffee adventure, or I could find a spot under one of the palm trees outside and strategize on my next move. Was there a better option other than playing drunk and pretending to be on the search for my glasses? Should I review the blueprints again? Or go over Natalie's instructions one more time?

No, Annie.

At some point, you have to stop.

It was true. Overthinking it or coming up with a last-minute change of plans wasn't smart or strategic.

I decided to wander through the book hall again. Concentrating on a panel was out of the question. I was too wound up to sit still, and it wouldn't hurt to take another look at the vendor displays. There was so much to see that I'd likely missed items that would sell well in the store on my first pass.

Upbeat music played overhead. It sounded like the soundtrack from *Notting Hill*, which made me smile. The organizers hadn't missed a beat. Everything about the convention was structured to make attendees feel like we were in another world —a bookish world.

The unique booth designs gave me so many ideas for the Secret Bookcase. One booth had created a secret passageway entirely out of books with signage reading: WELCOME TO THE LIBRARY OF SECRETS. They'd artfully arranged books in stacks and rows that appeared to form a secret passage with a hidden door. Mirrors and strategically positioned LED lights enhanced the illusion.

Another booth captured the essence of *The Secret Garden* with an arched trellis adorned with fake roses, ivy, and wildflowers. Stacks of books were nestled among garden benches, flower pots, and watering cans. They were peddling ceramic planters shaped like book stacks, garden tools with literary quotes, and custom seed packets with book branding like "Mystery Blooms." I leafed through the packets with their clever taglines—BURY YOUR SECRETS IN THE SOIL AND PLANT THE SEEDS OF SUSPENSE. Each packet was filled with forget-me-nots, lavender, and cosmos.

I could already imagine a summer display with the whimsical garden treats. Hal had floated the idea of offering high tea in the English garden, and I knew these items would be the perfect accompaniment to showcase in the Foyer and Sitting Room. The boxed sets of mysteries with loose-leaf tea put me over the edge. They would pair perfectly with the Book Crush candles I'd seen earlier, too.

I texted Hal.

> High tea is happening.

He responded immediately with a tea emoji and five photos of Professor Plum.

> I'll get my cravat and top hat ready. Professor Plum is quite smitten with Caroline. They've been enjoying leisurely reading time and naps. Hope the convention is going well. Any news on the accident? Sending my love. Hal.

I smiled and shook my head. Hal always signed off his texts with his name, even though Fletcher and I had explained it wasn't necessary. It had come to be one of my favorite things.

I responded to thank him for the pics and explained that the "accident" had turned into a full-fledged murder investigation. He responded with a barrage of questions. I answered them all and reassured him that Fletcher and I were fine and assisting the local police.

After our text exchange, I placed an order with the owner of the shop. Then I took a minute to sketch out a sample menu— mushroom and spinach mini quiches, egg salad sandwiches, lobster rolls, butter scones with jam and clotted cream, blueberry tarts, panna cotta cups, hazelnut petit fours, and chocolate mousse. I knew I could rope Pri and her team at Cryptic to cater the tea.

I felt lighter, having done something productive for the bookstore and gotten out of my head for a minute. The feeling didn't last long because I spotted Serena and Phillip deep in conversation near the exit doors. Actually, "conversation" wasn't the right word choice—it looked much more like an argument.

Serena dragged Phillip out of the book hall, hissing under her breath.

I followed them outside.

Serena looked like she was on the warpath. She marched to a secluded cluster of palm trees at the far end of the property. Phillip raced after her like an eager puppy dog.

Our earlier chat replayed in my head, and it didn't take long for me to put the pieces of Phillip's cagey clues together— Serena Highbourn was the client he was desperate to land. Of course.

I crept as close as I could, keeping out of sight thanks to one of the cabanas' blue-and-white-striped awnings.

It wasn't hard to hear. Serena was practically screaming.

"I told you, it's a no. No, Phillip." Serena's voice was laced with fury.

"But hear me out." He reached for her and then pulled his arm back close to his chest, trying to keep his composure. "I can offer you more than you realize."

"It's done. It's over." She made a slicing motion across her neck. "How many times do I have to tell you no before you'll listen? Is English a struggle for you?"

"I don't understand. What changed?" His voice cracked slightly, a clear edge of desperation breaking through. His words hung heavy in the air as he searched Serena's face, almost begging for clarity.

"Do I need to spell it out for you?"

"Yes, please. I don't get it. We discussed every detail of your contract. Why back out now?" His tone was pleading, as if he were grasping for an answer—any answer.

She cleared her throat and stared at her nails as if already bored with the conversation. "You couldn't seriously believe that I was entertaining your offer? Me, Serena Highbourn. Phillip, you're not a spring chicken. You're no dewy-eyed, overly enthusiastic young editor who believes he's going to change the world one book at a time. You know this business. I have dozens of offers. Higher offers. Better offers. I commend you for pleading your case, and I have every confidence you'll land a few names here and there, but not me. Sorry."

Nothing in her tone or body language was apologetic. Quite the opposite. I got the sense she was gloating and enjoying watching him squirm.

He smoothed his suit jacket. "Who came in with a higher offer?"

"This is highly unprofessional," Serena seethed, wagging her finger in his face. "If you have questions, you should take them up with my agent, not me. I'm doing you a favor and kindness by letting you know. Consider it a courtesy after all these years together in the industry."

"This isn't courtesy. You lied to me, Serena." Phillip was

losing control. He took off his jacket and tossed it over his shoulder. "Twenty-four hours ago, we shook hands. You said you were eager for a new chapter and ready for more creative control. This is out of the blue. It doesn't make sense."

"A handshake isn't a contract. Surely, you're not this naïve, Phillip. Pull yourself together and have a little self-respect. This is downright embarrassing." She tossed her hair to one side and walked away.

Phillip stood dumbfounded.

I waited for a minute until Serena returned inside to speak with him. "Are you okay? I overheard a snippet of your conversation."

He threw his jacket on the ground and pounded his fist into the trunk of a nearby palm so hard it caused it to sway. Then he shook his fingers like he'd hurt himself. "God, I hate that woman. She's the worst."

"Is she the client you were telling me about?" I asked gently.

He continued to fan his fingers. "Yeah. We made a deal. It was ironclad, and let me tell you, she came out ahead in every aspect of what I was offering her—complete creative control, TV and film rights, audio, world translation rights—everything was in her favor. Everything. A huge advance. I had to mortgage my house to come up with the money. We were in alignment. She's frustrated with her current publishing house and doesn't feel they're doing enough to promote her or her books. She used me. She must have used my offer as leverage to renegotiate her contract. That's underhanded and wrong."

"How did you find out she changed her mind?" I was most interested in his physical responses. The palm tree didn't deserve his rage. He could have seriously damaged it or his hand. In fact, I was curious if he'd broken a finger when punching the poor tree. This violent outburst could be a sign of his emotional instability and might point to him being the killer.

TWENTY-THREE

Phillip's cheeks turned a deep crimson. He rubbed the hand he'd used to assault the tree, massaging his bruised fingers tenderly. "Serena's agent called me about an hour ago. I was in a panel session, so I couldn't answer the call. I figured he was sharing the good news that we had a signed contract, but when I listened to the voicemail, he apologized and thanked me for my time and then proceeded to inform me that Serena had a last-minute change of heart and decided to accept another offer."

"It sounds like you believed she was serious about signing with you."

"She gave me no indication otherwise." Phillip sounded incredulous as his voice grew louder. "We had dinner last night. She told me it was done. She'd made her decision and was signing with me. We strategized and discussed my ideas for cover design and marketing for her work in progress. I can't believe she would do this to me. It's low, even for her."

"What do you mean, *even* for her?" I paid close attention to his body language. The color spreading along his neck and cheeks was a clear sign of his anger.

"Serena is ruthless. She'll do whatever it takes to get a story or get ahead." He had calmed down some, but a lingering tension remained. The occasional flicker of agitation on his face betrayed the calmer façade he was trying to maintain. "Her reputation precedes her. I should have known she'd screw me in the end. It's my own fault."

"I'm not familiar enough with the process. Is it common to have an author change their mind at the last minute?"

"Sure. Yeah. That's the nature of the beast, especially when a book goes to auction or an author like Serena makes it known she's on the market again, but this is different. She calculated her every move. Dinner last night was to garner ideas—my ideas—she can take to her publishing house and force them to implement. God, I'm a fool. I never should have trusted her." He pounded his fist into his palm, forgetting about his injury. A burst of pain flashed across his face.

"And you have no recourse since the contract wasn't signed." My glasses fogged up a bit. I removed them and used my sleeve to clear away the condensation.

"Nope." He smacked his lips together as he shook his head. "Nothing. This is going to ruin me financially. I was counting on my cut of her royalties and signing bonus for audio, foreign translations, and film. I'm not sure how much longer I'll be able to keep the doors open."

That sounded dire.

The pool area hummed to life as people trickled outside for the evening party. The band launched into an upbeat set, and beach balls sailed through the air. It was a strange juxtaposition to be having such a serious conversation with Phillip in such a carefree atmosphere.

Had Phillip put all his eggs into one basket? That didn't seem like a savvy business plan from a man who had spent years in the publishing industry. I wondered what his client list looked like. Did he have any other high-profile authors? Come to think of it, how many authors had he signed? And how—if at all—did this tie in with Fox's murder?

Was there more to their history?

If Fox was the reason Phillip's prior publishing company went bankrupt, could he have held a grudge? I'd seen his anger boil over firsthand. What if that combination had sparked? A theory began to take shape. Phillip could have plotted out Fox's murder, seeking revenge for his past financial losses. If that were the case, was Serena Highbourn in danger?

"What about your other authors?" I asked, putting my glasses back on.

Phillip kicked his jacket. "Good question. I might have to be the bearer of bad news."

"How many books have you published?" Our conversation was serving as a reminder that I needed to look into his background, too. Unless Fletcher had already done so. My bet was on Fletcher. He was a machine when it came to research.

He reached down, grabbed his coat, and brushed it off. "Look, I gotta go. I have serious damage control to do." He winced sharply, struggling to slide his jacket over his arm. His hand trembled slightly, and when he finally managed, it was impossible to miss the sight of his two bruised and swelling knuckles. They were already darkening to a deep, painful shade of eggplant. He had injured them more than he was letting on.

What else was he masking?

After he left, I did a quick search on my phone to see what I could find about his newly formed publishing house and current client list. My search returned a handful of articles announcing his new venture, a press release about his storied publishing history, and submission information for literary agents. I browsed his website, which was sparse, to say the least. The client section was blank with a COMING SOON notice.

Interesting.

Had Phillip signed a single author?

Something was off about the site. I couldn't put my finger on it, but it didn't feel legit. It was like he slapped a placeholder up with a bio, a lot of fluff, and no substance.

What was his business strategy?

To land Serena Highbourn?

Was an author of her caliber enough to keep an entire publishing house afloat? I still couldn't shake the feeling I was missing another connection between him and Fox.

I gave it a rest and went to find a spot to sit down. Luckily, a poolside table opened up as I passed by so I snagged it and texted the group chat to let them know I was staking my claim and where to find me.

Fletcher arrived first, carrying two glasses of pink lemonade. "I thought you might enjoy an afternoon refresher. They're serving pink lemonade—your weakness."

"Weakness might be a stretch, but I do love an ice-cold glass or two in the summer."

"Glass or two? Annie, I've seen you drink lemonade by the gallon. It's an addiction."

I furrowed my brow and gladly accepted the drink. "If you want to talk addiction, let's wait until Pri and Liam show up, jacked up on caffeine." It was sweet that Fletcher paid such close attention. It wasn't like I went around professing my love for it, but pink lemonade had a special place in my heart. My parents owned and ran a small family diner when I was growing up, which meant my afternoons were spent in a red vinyl booth doing my homework, reading, and drinking pink lemonade that my mom would finish off with a splash of fizzy water and a raspberry, strawberry, or lemon slice. On Fridays and weekends, I got to upgrade my lemonade to a milkshake.

"I'll drink to that." He raised his glass in a toast. "Any new developments since our last mind meld?"

"Yes. Quite a few, in fact." I pulled out my phone to review my notes. "Laurel tracked me down and explained her side of the story."

"Is there any merit to it?" Fletcher kicked an errant beach ball back to a group of partygoers nearby.

"She seems sincere, and her story checks out, but I'm not ready to absolve her yet." I gave him the shortened version of our discussion. "Oh, I also ordered a bunch of garden items for the store—I made the executive decision that the summer tea is a go. Also, did you see the book-map booth?"

"Did I see it? I bought it out, Annie. Book maps." He threw his hand to his forehead. "And a garden party is perfectly fine by me. Hal will be thrilled. He's been asking me nearly daily if we've thought it."

"Good. I'm glad you agree, and I have one more juicy piece of information to share." I told him about eavesdropping on Serena and Phillip's conversation and Phillip's outburst. "Right before you got here, I was doing a quick search. Have you looked into the house or his background?"

He frowned and made a ticking sound, waving his index finger like a metronome. "Have I done background research into each of our suspects? Annie, please. It's me. Your loyal Sherlock."

I grinned. "Sorry. I never doubted you. Everything's been so busy I feel like I've barely had a second to process anything."

"I'll give you a pass this time, but never again." He narrowed his eyes and then chuckled. "In all seriousness, I meant to mention this earlier, but the day slipped away from me, too. As far as I've been able to determine, Phillip doesn't have any clients. There was buzz—no, that's too generous— perhaps tepid press coverage when he announced he was striking out on his own over a year ago, but since then—crickets. His website has remained static. No author announcements. No staff announcements. No partnership announcements. Nothing."

"Okay, that's what I thought."

"It's odd and certainly not the behavior of an editor eager to build his client list and establish himself as an upcoming new publishing house. It doesn't add up."

"Agreed. His website almost feels fake."

"Fake. Hmm." Fletcher strummed his fingers on his chin. "I hadn't considered that, but it's the same placeholder page he launched with the announcement. He could be an abysmally poor marketer, or maybe he's been actively trying to land authors and failing?"

"If he isn't well-versed in marketing, you would think he would hire someone to do that piece of the business for him. Even in a small publishing house, there is always a marketing person. I wonder if he's been singularly focused on Serena Highbourn this entire year."

"Isn't that a long time to go after a client?"

"Yeah." I took a sip of the lemonade. A flood of diner memories came rushing to the front of my mind. The smell of the grease from the fryer. The jukebox. The black-and-white-checkered floors. The milkshake machine. Eating cheeseburgers and corn dogs. The regulars who would ask me about school while I had my nose in a Nancy Drew novel or was trying to put together a five-hundred-piece puzzle. My childhood had been small in terms of my circle, but I liked it that way.

"She is a big name," Fletcher said. "But one author a publishing house does not make. Or does it?"

"Good question. I feel like everything is connected, and we're missing the right critical piece that ties it together."

"Annie, Fletcher, we come bearing coffee!" Pri danced over to the table with a bag of aromatic beans.

Liam trailed after her, moving with an effortless ease. He looked devilishly handsome in his light khaki slacks and pale green shirt. The color made his eyes even more striking. As he approached, our gazes met—just for a moment—but it was enough. A slow, knowing smile passed between us before he sat beside me. Simply having him nearby made everything feel better, manageable, like the world didn't have to be a scary place filled with people like Logan Ashford.

I temporarily pushed questions about Phillip and Serena to the back of my mind while Pri and Liam recounted their coffee-tasting excursion. Maybe a little break from trying to fit the clues together would do the trick.

TWENTY-FOUR

"You would have loved it," Pri gushed as she passed out bags brimming with a variety of roasts, glossy chocolate-covered coffee beans, and sleek packets of mushroom coffee alternatives. Her energy was as invigorating as the products she was sharing. "We didn't have a miss, did we, Liam? No skips. The vibes at each of the coffee shops we visited were immaculate. Immaculate." She ripped open a bag of chocolate-covered beans and popped a handful in her mouth.

Liam dropped into the chair beside her, a knowing smirk playing on his lips as he patted her shoulder. "Go easy on those, my friend; you're still buzzing like a live wire."

That was the theme of the weekend, I thought to myself.

I tore open a bag of beans and tossed a couple in my mouth. They had a delightful contrast of texture and flavors. The smooth outer layer of chocolate melted instantly in my mouth. Its creamy sweetness gave way to the bitter crunch of the roasted bean inside. "These are delish."

Liam reached for a craft bag of coffee with handwritten tasting notes written in black Sharpie. "This was my personal favorite. It's a roast from an artisan bakeshop in Oregon. Every blend was nuanced and subtle with earthy and nutty tones and then a sharpness from the caffeine. I already emailed them to ask about wholesale for the pub. We don't get a ton of coffee drinkers, but I always want our nonalcoholic options to be top-notch, and this blend will make a mean non-alcoholic Irish coffee."

Pri bit down into another bean. "Agreed. I have a radical idea that we could rotate different roasters each month. In addition to our house blends, kind of like rotating taps at Stag Head. Wouldn't that be fun? It would allow our regulars to sample coffee from the West Coast and maybe even beyond."

"I love that idea." I savored the decadent intensity of the chocolate bean.

"That's just the tip of the iceberg." Pri's foot bounced as she presented a lengthy list of potential new ideas for Cryptic. "I'm thinking coffee passports, where customers get a stamp for every blend they try and then a free coffee once they fill up their passports. Brew-your-own-adventure nights where customers can learn to brew using various methods like Chemex and Aero-Press, and then they get to take home samples of their favorite beans from the session." Her speech became more rapid and enthusiastic as she gained steam. "Liam and I discussed a coffee and cocktails crossover night where we introduce coffee-based cocktails and mocktails, like smoked bourbon coffee old fashioned with cold brew, simple syrup, chocolate bitters, and orange peel."

"Don't forget the smoked woodchips," Liam said. "That's my department. I bring the booze and the smoke effects."

"Theatrics are always welcome," Pri replied. Then she looked at Fletcher and me. "You two are part of my total world coffee domination plan. What do you say to a Mystery Bean of the Month?"

"I say yes." I nodded enthusiastically.

"Yep, me too," Fletcher agreed.

"I haven't even told you what it is." Pri frowned.

"You had me at mystery," I teased.

She rolled her eyes. "At least let me try to sell you on the idea."

I smiled and waved my hand over the coffee haul. "The floor is yours."

"Thank you." She tipped her head in my direction. "As I was saying, imagine a Mystery Bean of the Month. Each month, we'll pair a book with beans. I'm not a book expert, obviously. I'll leave that to the two of you." She paused and rifled through the coffee samples until she landed on a shiny pink-and-green bag and then read us the description. "Take this, for example. It's floral-heavy. Lots of notes of hay, peapods, peaches, and grapefruit. You pick a garden-themed book, and we bundle them together for the month. Or it could be a dark roast paired with a noir. I don't know any noir titles off-hand, but you get the point."

"*The Maltese Falcon*," Fletcher interjected.

"Never read it, but yeah, sure. That's perfect. Customers could get clue cards with tasting notes, facts about the growing region, and maybe literary references. The possibilities are endless."

I clapped three times. "I'm impressed, and I'm so bummed we didn't get to tag along on your outing. It sounds highly productive."

Pri extended her hands, exaggerating a slight tremble as she grinned. "And the caffeine? Totally manageable. No problem. Look, my hands are as steady as a surgeon's."

Everyone cracked up.

"Anyway, enough about me." She exhaled and sank into her chair. "Let's get to the good stuff. Annie, lay it on me. Every. Single. Detail."

I washed the chocolate-covered coffee beans down with a

sip of lemonade. Big mistake. My mouth puckered at the combination. I made a face.

"Uh-oh, that bad?" Liam looked concerned.

"No. It went better than I anticipated, but I don't recommend pink lemonade and coffee beans. Bad combo." I stuck out my tongue and scrunched my forehead.

"Thanks for the heads-up." He tapped two fingers against his temple in a subtle salute before sliding his arm around the back of his chair.

I recounted my afternoon like a sports announcer, delivering a play-by-play breakdown of each minute.

Pri chomped on her fingernails when I finished. "I'm not sure what to think. Don't get me wrong, Annie, I'm not doubting your skills, but your point about Logan potentially using this to set you up is a very real possibility."

"Agreed." Liam's lips thinned into a narrow line as he nodded. "You're not going in alone tonight. It's out of the question. I'm coming with you."

"For sure." I nodded seriously. "I want you to come with me. Fletcher and I have already discussed it. He pitched me on the drunk glasses act, and I think it's a good idea."

Liam's eyes widened. "What?" He glanced from me to Pri and then Fletcher before landing his gaze back on me. "Did we hear that correctly, everyone? Annie Murray. The Annie Murray is agreeing to help without putting up a fight. Are you feeling okay?" He reached over to touch my forehead.

"I get it. I admit I've tended to be too stubborn and independent at times in the past, but no part of me trusts Logan Ashford. I'm not taking a single chance. Natalie's documents are within our reach. We need to get in, grab them, and get out."

Liam gave me a slow, measured, approving nod. I could almost see him processing what he was hearing in the moment. "Good. Well, that's settled, then. What's our evening plan?"

Fletcher checked his watch. "I'm off to Victor Moore's meetup before campus-surveillance duty. Consider it information gathering." He tapped his finger to his temple. "I'm hopeful some of the other suspects might attend. I imagine Theodore will go. Maybe Phillip. Regardless, I'll channel my inner Sherlock and report back later. Don't worry, I'll take off in plenty of time to do my surveillance of Silicon Summit Headquarters before the mission is a go."

He stood. I considered teasing him that it wasn't a stretch for him to channel his inner Sherlock. That was practically his personality, but I could tell he was focused and on a mission. I knew what it felt like to be in that mode, and I didn't want to distract him.

"Wait, real quick before you leave, Liam and I swung by Serena's signing," Pri said, pulling out Serena's latest tell-all and flipping to the signature page. "I got her to inscribe this copy for Cryptic. We tried to ask her a few questions about Fox, but she didn't budge—not an inch." Pri shot a glance to Liam.

He nodded in agreement, absentmindedly loosening a button on his light blue shirt. "Nothing." The early evening sun cast a warm glow across his skin, highlighting the sharp angle of his jaw and the faint shadow of stubble. Everything about him only added to his effortless charm and made a tiny part of me want to run off into the sunset with him and forget about my wild plan to try to bring down Logan Ashford. He backed up Pri as he shook his head. "Seriously. Not a word. She was a vault."

"That's disappointing." Fletcher started to leave, but Pri held up a finger.

"Wait, there is something, though. I overheard her say she had another listening session at the bar."

"What's a listening session?" Fletcher asked, looking at me. "Is that a new literary term?"

I shrugged. "Not that I've heard of. She said a listening session? Not a signing?" I clarified, turning to Pri.

"Yep. I'm positive, and that's the weird part. I don't think she realized we were there when she said it. She was super flustered, spilled her water everywhere, and then made a big production out of signing my book and pretending like nothing happened. I mean, she does have *people* to clean up her messes, but still, it was bizarre. Am I right, Donovan?"

Liam nodded, catching my eye and letting his gaze linger for a minute. "Agreed. It was odd."

I appreciated his steadfast support and how invested he was in this case, too. A server passed by. I reached for another glass of lemonade. It was like I couldn't get enough liquid in my body. I recognized the stress response, and tried not to let it bother me. If I wasn't stressed right now, that's when I should be worried.

"Hmm. I'll check the program. Maybe she's doing a special event," Fletcher said, moving toward the doors. "I'll catch up with you later."

"Yeah, I should go, too." Pri gathered her coffee samples and stood up. "I promised Penny I would call and show her my coffee stash. I guess it's just you two lovebirds. I'll be on standby and ready for my role at a moment's notice. I have Dr. Caldwell's number saved in my favorites, and I intend to give her a play-by-play and have her sound the alarm if necessary."

Everyone had a role in the next phase of the operation.

Pri would relay updates to Dr. Caldwell in real time. Fletcher planned to survey the campus prior to Liam and my arrival. He would check the parking lot to assess how many staff, if any, were still on site and be on the lookout for anything unusual.

"I guess that leaves you and me," Liam said after Pri left, reaching for my hand, his fingers threading through mine in an easy, unspoken gesture of solidarity. It felt natural, like we were a team, facing whatever came next. He squeezed my hand before glancing at me with his sultry eyes. "Dinner? A drink to take the edge off?"

"Dinner sounds good." I brought my lemonade with us, sipping it slowly to quench my thirst and ease my nerves. Truthfully, I doubted I could eat much. We were mere hours away from closing the biggest case of my life.

TWENTY-FIVE

"Would you like to eat here or go out somewhere?" Liam asked.

"The hotel bar looks nice, and I'd rather be close. I don't have a reason, exactly. Nerves, I guess." I raised the lemonade glass. "I'm going to turn into a lemon at this point, but something about the puckery taste is helping to calm me down. Weird, right?"

"Understandable." Liam put his arm around me. "If you weren't nervous, I'd be worried. This is a big deal."

"Yeah, I was just telling myself the same thing." I swallowed the fear bubbling up in me. I wasn't as worried about getting caught or Logan setting a trap for me as I was not finding the evidence. Without proof, Logan would remain free.

"Hey, can we take a quick detour upstairs? I want to check Scarlet's journals one more time. Something finally clicked, and I think there's a chance she may have left me a clue."

"What are we waiting for? Let's go." He ushered me toward the elevators.

In our room, I set my lemonade on the nightstand and spread Scarlet's journals out over the bed, concentrating on her last one. It was a spiral-bound notebook with an illustration of a tabby cat on the cover—a gift I'd given her after she'd brought Professor Plum home weeks before graduation. I'd read through the journal too many times to count, but suddenly, I had fresh eyes. I wasn't trying to decipher her case notes and drawings. I was looking for an Easter egg.

"Can I help?" Liam asked, sitting on the end of the bed.

I motioned to her older journals. "Feel free to look through those. Let me know if you see an Easter egg."

Liam gave me a quizzical look. "What kind of Easter egg are we talking about?" He propped himself on the edge of the bed and reached for a journal with flowers.

"She used to make mazes and puzzles for me to solve. All this time I've pored through these thinking they contained the evidence, but on my way to Silicon Summit Partners, I had an aha moment that she might have left a sign about *where* to find the evidence." I licked the tip of my finger and leafed through her familiar doodles and notes. "But the problem is I've studied these journals to the point I can recite what's on each page by memory. Could I have missed it?"

"One way to find out," he said, opening the pretty floral pages containing a snapshot of Scarlet's short-lived life. "I've got fresh eyes if nothing else."

We spent the next forty minutes searching for an Easter egg or clue that may or may not exist. But nothing new surfaced.

"Maybe this is a lost cause," I said to Liam with a sigh, reaching for my lemonade. My hand slipped. A splash of the pink liquid spread across the worn page of Scarlet's journal, instantly soaking into the paper.

"Oh no!" I jumped up. "No, no, no. What have I done?" I frantically dabbed the pages with the comforter. My heart sank as I watched the ink blur at the edges.

"Hair dryer?" Liam suggested, pointing to the bathroom.

"Yeah, good idea." I clutched Scarlet's journal and rushed to the bathroom. I turned the heat on the hairdryer to its highest setting, hoping I might be able to dry the pages before the paper warped completely. Hot air fluttered the pages and filled the small bathroom with the scent of citrus.

Liam hovered near the door. "Is it working?"

"Maybe, I think so." I kept going, running the warm heat over each page.

Then something strange happened.

As the dryer baked the lemon-soaked pages, faint dark lines appeared, like a ghostly ink rising from the grave.

I froze. My eyes widened. "Are you seeing this?" I waved Liam closer.

Was I imagining things or were those more than just random smudges?

I tilted the journal. The marks sharpened, forming words.

"Oh. My. God, Liam—look!" The realization of what I was seeing sent a shiver down my spine. "Scarlet wrote something in an invisible ink. I remember this from a course in college, but it never dawned on me. There are special inks—iron salt and copper sulfate ink that react to acids, like my lemonade, and heat." I paused to catch my breath. "This is it, Liam! This is it!"

He leaned over my shoulder to get a closer look.

I pointed to the tiny sketch; at first glance it seemed to be nothing more than a doodle. But now under the heat's gentle coaxing, the faint lines had formed into something deliberate—a filing cabinet. It wasn't just a simple drawing. It was a code, a blueprint. Sharp arrows pointed to the bottom of the cabinet, and another sketch like an architect's schematics showed a compartment at the base. "I think there's something hidden in one of the filing cabinets," I said, my pulse thundering through my veins. "There's a whole bank of them in the HR offices... and in Logan's office." I traced the markings with my finger.

This wasn't random. This was her style. Leaving just

enough for me to follow but embedding it in plain sight—a clue only I could recognize.

The lemonade!

Of course, lemons activated the ink. Everything Scarlet did was by design. Our apartment was always stocked with lemonade. She must have known she was in danger and purposely hid the clue for me, assuming I would piece it together.

Sorry it took me so long, Scarlet.

I turned to Liam, my voice barely a whisper. "Now we know where we need to look."

I held the pages for him to see as my mind made furious connections. Her crisp arrows and compartment weren't just random markings. They reminded me of something I knew intimately—the secret bookcase in the Sitting Room.

Hiding in plain sight.

It was a classic Scarlet move. Another carefully placed breadcrumb, a puzzle piece, waiting for the right person to notice. She'd always been obsessed with Clue, riddles, and hidden compartments.

"This is her signature," I murmured. "Do you see it? One of the filing cabinets must have a hidden compartment, just like the bookstore."

"Funny that you ended up working at the Secret Bookcase, isn't it?" He tipped his head to the side and met my eyes.

"She wanted me to find this. And I finally have. I wish I had gotten here sooner, you know?"

"Hey, it took the time it needed. You found it now, which is all that matters." He leaned in, pausing before our lips met. His voice caught as he massaged my cheek with his thumb. "Annie, you constantly amaze me with your bravery and dedication. I'm sure you're right about this. I believe in you, and I will be with you every step of the way."

"Thanks," I managed to whisper before we kissed. His

confidence in me and Scarlet's sketch bolstered my resolve. I could do this. I was ready.

I packed Scarlet's journals away, and we returned downstairs, walking hand in hand through the conference area toward the front lobby.

Once again, the bar was packed with attendees enjoying literary-themed drinks and small plates. We waited to be seated. The hostess gave us a spot near the windows with a view of the pool and grounds. After placing our order, Liam reached for my hand and caressed my fingers.

"How are you doing, for real?"

A familiar knot tightened in my throat. I tried to force it down with a hard swallow, but it didn't work. "I'm scared."

He squeezed my hands. "That's normal."

"I'm not worried about me, but what if the evidence isn't there? What if someone found it? Or worse, what if Natalie is part of the conspiracy, and she's setting me up?"

"That thought never crossed my mind." Liam ran his teeth over his bottom lip. "Do you think that's a possibility?"

"Every possibility is on the table until I'm holding the evidence in my hands."

"Sure. Yeah." He released his grasp when our server delivered drinks and fresh bread to the table.

I was about to expand on the thought when I noticed Serena Highbourn seated at the bar, seemingly relaxed with a martini in hand and a pair of wireless earbuds tucked subtly into her ears. I caught snippets of her conversation with the bartender over the hum of chatter and clinking glasses around us. She maneuvered a tablet with one hand and kept tapping at her ear.

"What is it?" Liam started to turn around.

"Wait. Don't." I shook my head. "It's Serena Highbourn."

Serena had coerced the bartender into a conversation. She

appeared tipsy, rocking slightly on the stool and coming precariously close to spilling her cocktail.

The bartender recognized her. "Oh, you're the bestselling author. The Hollywood spy. How do you do it?"

"I'm a great listener." Serena wiggled her ear. "I have my ways."

Liam stared at me. "What is happening? You're transfixed."

I held a finger to my lips. "Hang on. I think it's all finally falling into place. I'm having another aha moment." A realization dawned on me. Serena wasn't just casually chatting. She was using the earbuds to eavesdrop on conversations. "Her listening sessions—like you and Pri heard. That's how she does it!"

"Does what? What are we talking about?" Liam sounded utterly lost.

"Sorry." I lowered my voice. "It's Serena. She's listening in on everyone's conversations here in the bar. When you heard her mention a listening session, she wasn't talking about a panel or a conference event—she was speaking literally. She's eavesdropping right now. That must be one of her strategies for obtaining gossip and insider information. I don't think those are normal earbuds. She must have them connected to an app on her phone. She keeps glancing at her phone and making small adjustments like she's controlling the mic's sensitivity or range."

"Are you serious?" Liam stole a quick glance at Serena.

I nodded. "Hold on."

Two guys I recognized from Victor's session were seated next to us, at least thirty feet away from Serena—well out of earshot. "This convention is cutting-edge, isn't it?" the guy said to his tablemate. "I just participated in a VR-gaming experience. The visuals were so good I thought it was going to short-circuit when they connected it to a PC."

"Look," I said to Liam, motioning toward the bar.

Serena batted her eyes at the bartender in a weird attempt

at flirtation —or maybe distraction. "Funny, isn't it, how people always think they're going to short-circuit their systems? It's not as fragile as they think."

I frowned.

How was Serena well-versed in the fragility of the systems?

It didn't add up.

And how had she heard the conversation at the table next to us?

My theory had to be right. I couldn't believe it took me this long to put it together, but in fairness, I had been preoccupied with Logan Ashford and Silicon Summit Partners.

Time to test it.

I leaned back and spoke louder, emphasizing each word to Liam as if English wasn't his first language. "Serena couldn't have done it—she doesn't even know how to use technology, right?" I deliberately used her name as bait.

Serena interrupted her own conversation from across the bar, letting out a condescending chuckle. "Ha! You'd be surprised what people can learn when motivated. Technology is nowhere near as complicated as people like to make it seem. You just need money and the right experts, and anything is possible."

The bartender looked perplexed. "Yeah, okay. You want another?"

"Detective Greene mentioned she's on her way here to make an arrest," I said, intentionally making my voice even louder and wiggling my eyebrows at Liam. "Apparently, Serena was the mastermind behind Fox's murder. I can't believe I missed it. I pegged her as someone who resisted technology, but it turns out she rigged the device to kill him."

"Really?" Liam played his part perfectly, staring at me as if he were equally perplexed by the possibility.

"Check! Check!" Serena demanded, stealing a glance over her shoulder at our table as she flagged down the bartender.

"It's her. I've got her," I whispered to Liam. "Be right back."

Serena motioned wildly for the bartender to hurry. "Check, I need the check, you idiot." She was trying to hightail it out of the bar before I confronted her.

I approached the bar casually and gestured to her earbuds. "Nice tech you've got there. Those are wireless, aren't they? I'm curious how they work. My business partner and I are in the market for our private detective agency. Is it tricky to sync them with the mic with all the background noise here?"

Serena froze. "I have no idea what you're talking about." Her hand instinctively touched her ear. Her calm demeanor faded as she tried to brush it off. "These? They're just for music. I can't even—"

I cut her off. "For someone who claims to be a Luddite, you certainly seem to have a handle on advanced tech. Makes me wonder what else you've been hiding."

Serena reached for her drink, threw it into my face, and broke for the exit.

My glasses had protected my eyes, but the bar dissolved into a blurry haze. Liquid streaked down my lenses, distorting the view and making everything warp like I was peering through murky water. "Stop her," I yelled, tearing off my glasses and rubbing them on my sleeve.

I blinked, trying to see if she'd escaped.

The bar went quiet. People turned in their seats and jumped to their feet. I could barely make out her shadowy silhouette sprinting toward the door when someone dashed in front of her and barred her way.

"Got her!" Liam yelled from the floor.

I tucked my glasses in my purse—I didn't need them for my next mission anyway. Gin trickled down my cheek and dripped onto my shirt. My view was still out of focus, but improved. I grabbed my phone from the table and called Detective Greene to let her know we'd apprehended Serena Highbourn.

"On my way. I'm not far," Detective Greene said with urgency. "Don't let her leave."

Liam played the part of guard, keeping a strong arm on Serena while we waited for reinforcements. He moved her to an empty table while I informed the bartender and staff that the authorities were coming. She was surrounded. There was no chance of an escape now.

"How did you do it—rewire the Headset?" I asked, sitting across from her, and wiping my face with a napkin.

"Easy." She smirked. "I don't understand how anyone bought the load of bull that Fox Andrews was a tech genius. Far from it. It was simple. Move a few wires, activate it with my phone, and boom."

I shuddered.

Serena didn't appear the least bit remorseful. If anything, she came across as proud. "He deserved everything he had coming. That liar, thief, and cheat. I've poured blood, sweat, and tears into this career, establishing myself. I never betray my sources, and I never reveal my methods."

"You were concerned Fox would pilfer your contacts?"

"No. Not in the slightest. No one in my inner circle would dare say a word to him. These are celebrities and billionaires. They have people who vet everyone from their dog walkers to their private chefs. Fox had no way in."

I was confused. Serena's motive for wanting him dead had been clear in my mind up until this point. I was about to ask her for clarification, but it wasn't necessary. She kept talking, almost as if no one was in the room with her.

"He learned about my secret. Like you, he caught me listening to a heated conversation between two A-list actors, and he approached me about a partnership. You see, I developed this special app with the help of some very clever and very discreet business associates. It's proprietary. Fox recognized the potential for mass-producing and turning a quick profit. He wasn't wrong about that. Could I have marketed the listening device? Absolutely. Would I? Never. Without these little beauties, I'd have limited access to information." She tapped her ear. "I've earned trust over the years, but a nice juicy nugget goes a long way to forcing people to spill their secrets. Fox was furious when I turned him down, and then he had the audacity to blackmail me."

"Blackmail you?" I caught Liam's eye. He motioned to keep her talking.

"He gave me a choice—I could either partner with him, or he would go to the press and write an exposé detailing my tactics and insider secrets. He was true to his word. He showed me a copy of his hit piece. That was a fatal error. Did he think I would sit idly by and watch my life's work blow up before me? Ha! Hardly. He was arrogant and ill-informed. He assumed that because I have gray hair, I would cave to his demands. Little did he know, the wheels were already set in motion for his demise. It took two phone calls. Five hours later, I had a prototype of his ridiculous Headset and an app on my phone. I waited for the exact moment and clicked one button. Bam."

There it was again.

She was almost giddy recounting how she had killed him.

Her confession in front of a bar full of people was also going to make Detective Greene's job much easier.

I was relieved to have solved Fox's murder. Serena would soon be arrested and behind bars before the night was over.

Now I had one final job to finish.

TWENTY-SIX

The air wasn't particularly cool, but I couldn't shake the chill sending quivers down my body.

"I don't want to get in your head, Annie," Liam said as we walked to the Silicon Summit Partners campus. "But if you have any reservations, or if you pick up the slightest hint that it feels off, we can turn around, okay?"

"I know." I agreed to appease him when, in reality, there was no chance I was bailing, and we both knew it.

"I had to say it for my own sanity." Liam sounded hesitant, as if he wanted to say more, but stopped himself.

We walked the rest of the way in silence. A buzzy, anticipatory sense of excitement—or maybe dread—rushed through me. I focused on putting one foot in front of the other and steeling my gaze at the opaque moon casting an ethereal glow on the sidewalk. I could almost smell the fear radiating off me, but I forced it away as I drank in the cool air, trying not to hold my breath.

I texted Fletcher at our prearranged meeting spot at the far end of campus. He and Pri were staking out the main drive from a safe distance. "Now we wait," I said to Liam.

"He'll come through."

I didn't doubt Fletcher's abilities. We agreed to wait out of sight until Fletcher texted to give us the all-clear.

My heart thudded against my chest like it was trying to break free. Time seemed to slow and speed up at once. The sinking sunlight hit the glass windows of the four-story building, casting shimmery shadows on the empty grounds. Occasionally, a car would drive by on the street, disturbing the peace, but otherwise, there was no sign of activity short of a gust of breeze through the palm trees every once in a while.

Why is Fletcher taking so long?

Is something wrong?

Did he get caught?

"He'll text," Liam said gently as if reading my mind.

I didn't want to give any credence to the swarm of negative thoughts threatening to take over. If we were to succeed in our mission, I had to remain calm.

"Mm-hmm," I mumbled, standing on my tiptoes to see if I could spot Fletcher in the growing twilight. Then I checked my watch. He should have checked in by now. Fletcher was nothing if not punctual.

"Would you feel better if you text him again?" Liam suggested.

"No, I'll be patient." I gave him a sheepish grin. "It's not always my strong suit."

"Really? You? Murray? I'm shocked. And here this entire time, I thought you were the model of patience."

I punched him in the shoulder and cracked a smile. I knew he was teasing me, and I was grateful. It helped break at least a tiny piece of the tension I was holding.

"That's more like it." His strong jawline sharpened even further when he smiled, as though he'd been expertly sculpted from clay, each angle perfectly defined.

My heart fluttered again with a different kind of energy.

Before I could come up with a clever retort, my phone vibrated. I had already turned it onto silent mode on the off chance that one of the guards was sweeping the entire perimeter.

> Sorry. Victor was talking my ear off. Then word spread that Serena was arrested. Is it true?

I had nearly forgotten about Serena since we'd set off. Had that really only been thirty or forty minutes ago?

> Yep.

> I had a bunch of intel to share on Victor that's not necessarily relevant now. Fill you in later. Coast is clear. No cars in the back lot. No sign of activity inside. One guard at the main gate. You're a go.

> Thanks.

> We're standing by. Good luck.

> Get 'em, Annie

Pri added with a strong-arm emoji.

> I'm ready to update Dr. Caldwell.

"We're a go," I told Liam, showing him Fletcher's text. My entire body felt like it was humming with a tangible energy I couldn't contain.

Liam didn't move. "Last chance to change your mind."

"Nope." I shook my head vehemently. "You?"

"I'm in. All in. All in, Annie. Always." He held my gaze with an intense sincerity that made me want to leave the world, Scarlet's murder, and everything else behind and collapse in his arms.

"Thank you," I whispered, not trusting myself to say more. I gulped in a breath and looped my arm through his, deliberately staggering a bit to sell the act. It helped that I couldn't see very well without my glasses. "Lllleeettt's dooo thisss," I said, drawing out the words and letting them fall out of my mouth like they were too heavy to hold.

My practiced drunk walk involved an uneven shuffle. I dragged my left foot along the pavement. As we approached the gate, I stumbled intentionally, clutching Liam's arm for support and giggling as if I found my clumsiness hilarious. "Oopsies, I tripped," I chirped too loudly.

"You okay?" Liam steadied me with his strong arm, holding me upright.

The guard stepped out of his booth, his hand immediately going to the walkie-talkie and Taser tethered to his waist.

I blinked slowly, as though trying to center my focus, my gaze darting around just enough to take in our surroundings and make sure he didn't have backup waiting nearby without looking too obvious. I gestured with my free hand, talking in nonsense, my sentence trailing off as if I'd lost my train of thought mid-word. "I need that... uh... thingy. Y'know, the... thing!"

Liam caught the guard's eye and nodded toward me. "She had an extra glass or two of champagne."

The guard scowled. "Not my problem. You're on private property."

"The thingy." I tapped the side of my eye, missing and poking my eyeball. "Ouch." I rubbed it with my fist. "I forgot them... inside."

Liam interpreted for me. "She forgot her glasses when she was here earlier. She didn't realize she'd left them behind until we were at dinner, and she can't see her hand in front of her face without them."

The guard stared at me skeptically, like he was trying to decide what to do with me. "You'll have to wait until normal business hours. The building will open again on Monday morning."

"Noooo!" I wailed, stretching my arms forward like a child grasping for a balloon bobbing away in the wind.

"She really can't see without her glasses. We're from out of town. She can't drive home without them." Liam was doing a remarkable job selling our case.

The guard removed his hand from his belt and shrugged. "Sorry. I don't have access to the building. Only staff with key cards can get in."

"Me." I raised my hand and waved. Then I started digging through my purse, making it look like bending over had thrown me off balance. I used Liam's arm to steady myself and yanked the key card out of my purse like I was holding a winning lottery ticket.

The guard studied the card, scowling as he looked from it to me and back again. "I don't recognize you. You don't work here."

"I do!" I clutched my chest and rocked from side to side in a little happy dance.

"She interviewed this afternoon," Liam explained. "That's when she accidentally forgot her glasses. She was so excited about landing the job. She must have taken them off when she was filling out the employment contract and left them behind. As you can see, we went out for a celebratory drink or two or three."

The guard hesitated. He frowned and handed me the key card. "You know where you left them?"

I pressed my lips together, nodding earnestly. "Yep. Yep. I know the exact spot."

The guard waited with a raised eye. "Where?"

"Oh, uh... yeah." I giggled again, throwing my hand over my mouth. "HR. In the office. On the... uh... what's it called? You know, the desk."

The guard exhaled. "Look, this is against protocol. Get in there, grab your glasses, and come right out, understood?"

"Thanks so much, man. Really appreciate it," Liam said, suddenly speaking bro code.

The guard shrugged and pressed the button to let us pass. "Be quick about it."

"I will, Officer." I saluted him and stumbled forward. "I can't believe it worked," I whispered to Liam. "He bought it."

"You could have a future in acting."

"Now, that is comical." I moved in a weaving, zigzagging pattern as if the ground beneath me was tilting, bumping into Liam and nearly knocking him off his feet. I had no idea if the guard was watching, but I wasn't breaking character. We weren't out of the woods yet.

TWENTY-SEVEN

I touched the key card to the door and heard the lock click open. I randomly pivoted and turned around, waving wildly at the guard, keeping my limbs loose and uncoordinated like I was a puppet with a few strings cut loose.

He had returned to his station.

"I hope he isn't reporting this," I said to Liam as I pushed the door open.

"We have to be quick. I think he bought our story, but we better move like our lives depend on it." He didn't say the quiet part out loud—our lives did depend on getting the evidence and getting out as quickly as possible.

"This way," I said to Liam, hurrying toward the elevators.

The glossy, sterile space felt eerie without anyone inside. The fading light outside trickled in through the windows, but I couldn't shake the ominous feeling that we were being watched. That was probably because we were being watched. Earlier, I noted at least a half dozen cameras strategically placed throughout the lobby. A few were mounted on the ceiling, while others were discreetly hidden near the artwork and plants. Regardless of whether the guard informed Logan or anyone else about our whereabouts, there would be tangible video evidence of us. We were being recorded right now.

What if Logan has a live feed?

I moved too quickly and halted abruptly as if I had forgotten where I was going. I paused in mid-step, squinting at my surroundings.

"Keep it up, Annie," Liam said under his breath.

I placed one foot in front of the other like I was balancing on a tightrope as I reached for the elevator call button. "Ding! Ding!"

The elevator doors opened.

I grabbed Liam for balance and dragged him inside. "So far so good."

He checked his phone. "No updates from Fletcher."

Fletcher was keeping an eye out for any unexpected arrivals. If a car pulled up to the gate, he would text us and let us know. Could that mean we were in the clear?

If Logan had been alerted that I was in the building, I had zero doubts he would drop everything and get here as fast as possible.

Liam typed with his thumb. "I'm double-checking just to be on the safe side."

We stepped off the elevator, and I resumed my routine, skipping forward playfully but stumbling on the slick floors and catching myself on the wall.

"Fletcher says, 'All quiet on the Western Front.'" Liam stuffed his phone back into his pocket. "I appreciate the historical reference."

"Never read it." I shook my head.

"What? That's a travesty. We'll have to remedy that once we're—" His voice caught.

"We're going to be fine." I squeezed his hand and dragged him forward. "This is it." I pointed to the Human Resources office. My body felt like it was floating. I could barely feel my fingers on the door handle as I turned it slowly, half expecting to find it locked. It turned with ease. "It's showtime."

Liam followed me inside and started to flip on the lights.

"We should leave those off," I said. "The guard knows I'm looking for my glasses, but he'll be able to see us. Even if he's not the sharpest tool in the shed, it won't take him long to realize I didn't leave my glasses in a secret compartment in a filing cabinet."

"Good point." Liam clicked on his flashlight app. "Let's get to it."

"I wish there weren't so many." I squinted and pointed to the bank of filing cabinets dominating the far wall. Eight imposing black cabinets stood side by side. Their surfaces were dull and scuffed. Each drawer had a sign holder, and most of them were filled with faded paper tags—that was a good sign. Wear and tear meant that these weren't brand-new, shiny cabinets. "If I'm right about Scarlet's invisible ink sketches, there should be a secret compartment in one of these, I'm guessing at the very back of the bottom drawer," I said, already dreading the daunting task of searching through the dark, cramped space.

"Process of elimination, I guess. You take that side. I'll start here?" Liam suggested, tugging on the farthest cabinet. "Uh-oh. We have a problem."

"What?" My heart sank.

"It's locked."

"Locked." I reached for the handle and tried the cabinet closest to me. "Crap. This one is locked, too."

We went down the row, systematically jiggling each one, hoping we might get lucky.

"Okay, plan B." I scanned the office, and my eyes landed on the desk where I had signed my employment contract earlier. There was no sign of my favorite purple glasses, but they were a small sacrifice for finding Scarlet's hidden files. I opened the drawers and began riffling through them. "There must be a key."

"Isn't this like plan Z at this point?" Liam positioned the flashlight so I could see. "Anything?"

"No." I heard the panic creeping into my tone. "What are we going to do?"

"Keep looking." He checked behind the filing cabinets and around the rest of the room.

This can't be our stopping point.

I closed my eyes, willing my pulse to slow and my mind to stop racing. I couldn't let the anxiety take hold. We had minutes at best. If that. And I didn't even know if the evidence was in this room. There was an entire building to consider.

I couldn't let fear paralyze me.

I fumbled around in the dark. "Can you shine more light right here?" I ran my fingers along the bottom of the drawer, tossing notepads and boxes of staples out of my way. "Here we go—keys!" I dangled a set of keys in triumph.

"Well done." Liam directed the flashlight toward the bank of filing cabinets. "Now, which one?"

We wasted no time. I went down the row and unlocked each of the filing cabinets.

I yanked a polished handle open and dropped to my knees.

There was nothing in the first or second.

"Anything?" I asked Liam, feeling hope starting to fade. We'd discussed the harsh reality that since Scarlet had hidden the evidence a decade ago, it was highly plausible that Silicon Summit Partners had upgraded their office furniture in the last ten years and that the filing cabinet containing the proof we desperately needed to convict Logan Ashford was gone. I'd opted not to entertain the possibility. Filing cabinets were practically indestructible and lasted for years. Plus, the company hadn't moved. If the headquarters had been relocated, it was much more likely they might have invested in new filing cabinets.

"No. I've struck out." Liam slammed the drawer shut and moved to the next.

"Liam, we don't have much time. Let's split up. I'll check these last few. You check Logan's office. It's on the third floor, right above us." I pointed to the ceiling. "It's the only other place I can imagine Scarlet hiding the evidence. I'm betting his office is probably locked, but it's worth a shot. We're not getting another chance like this."

"Annie, I don't know." He hesitated, checking his phone again.

"We don't have time to debate." I could hear the urgency in my voice. "It's either here or in Logan's office. We have minutes at best. Go! I'll meet you back in the lobby."

"Okay." Liam abandoned his filing cabinet, not bothering to close it as he took off in a sprint.

I moved on to the next filing cabinet.

Scarlet, show me.

I breathed deeply and reminded myself why we were here —for Scarlet.

I tugged the cabinet open and felt along the bottom of it.

Please, please let it be here.

It was as if my silent prayer was answered.

"Oh my God!"

At that moment, my phone buzzed with a text from Fletcher.

Abort! Abort! Five black SUVs just passed the guard station and are about to pull up to the front doors.

TWENTY-EIGHT

I sprang into action, flipping, snapping, and trying to open the hidden compartment.

Get out of there!

I yanked as hard as I could, feeling my muscles seize. There was no chance I was leaving without the evidence. It was here, I just had to get it.

I could hear the sounds of screeching tires and voices outside.

This is bad.

This is really bad.

A string of texts from Fletcher flooded my phone.

They're getting out of their SUVs.

Hurry.

You have to leave now!

Did you find it?

I'd studied the blueprints to know two exits were in the back. I just had to secure the documents. There was time. There had to be time. I used my entire body weight to try to pry the compartment open.

I was so close.

Breathe.

Focus.

I let my mind go still, concentrating on all the people who loved me and were cheering me on in this moment. I thought of Hal's steady guidance over the last few years and Dr. Caldwell's mentorship and faith in me. I pictured the Secret Bookcase and its cheery, warm hallways and cozy reading nooks, I imagined dinner outside under the stars at Penny's orchard, pictured strolling through Oceanside Park with Liam, and then I centered on Scarlet. I had known her better than anyone. This was my case to solve.

I'd read about special hidden compartments designed to open in unconventional ways—ones that required more than a key or a simple latch. At the Secret Bookcase, a single spine acted as a trigger, unlocking a concealed passage to a hidden room. Scarlet must have used something similar. She wouldn't have just tucked the evidence away for anyone to find.

But how did this one work?

She'd gone to great lengths to protect what she'd hidden. It only made sense that her hiding place wasn't giving up its secrets that easily.

Think, Annie.

Think like Scarlet.

They're coming!!!

Instead of prying or triggering the latch, I slid it to the left and then to the right. Like magic, the compartment swung open.

"I did it!" I said out loud to no one as I reached inside and pulled out a sealed envelope.

The elevator dinged, announcing its arrival.

I was out of time. Where was Liam?

There was no time to figure it out. I sprinted down the hallway, away from the elevator. Angry voices echoed behind me. Their footsteps were fast and heavy—the unmistakable scuff of shoes on the polished floors. Someone was running.

I clutched the envelope with a death grip, running as fast as my short legs would carry me.

I could feel Logan's henchmen closing.

I slipped through the door and found myself in a dark stairwell. I took the stairs two at a time, dropping my drunk act and ignoring the barrage of messages buzzing on my phone.

> Five SUVs, you guys. The place is surrounded.

When I got to the bottom, I froze and went silent.

Five SUVs meant Logan had brought reinforcements. They probably had every exit surrounded.

I was out of options.

My only choice was to confront Logan and buy enough time for the police to arrive. That was if he didn't shoot me on the spot. But what about Liam?

Where was he?

Had they already found him?

My intuition said that Logan wouldn't do anything rash. How would he explain two bodies? Two gunshots?

He couldn't explain that to the police. Liam and I weren't armed.

I texted Fletcher.

> Don't know where Liam is. Got split up. I'm going to confront Logan.

I opened the door with confidence.

As expected, a man dressed in black tactical gear stood at the ready, waiting for me. His stance was rigid and commanding. He aimed his Taser at me as he barked in an authoritative tone, "You're on private property. We'll have you arrested for breaking and entering."

"I'd like to speak with Logan." I wondered if my tone sounded calm. I felt oddly at ease.

The man kept his Taser pointed at me and reached for his walkie-talkie. "We've got her, sir."

The response came in too garbled for me to make out.

"The lobby?" the guard asked, his walkie-talkie crackling with static. "Be right there."

I frantically tried to assess how long it would take me to get out of the building safely if I tried to make a break for it.

I knew the answer.

I couldn't.

There was no chance of an escape now.

It was a lost cause.

There was only one way out, and that was through Logan Ashford.

"This way." The man motioned with the Taser.

I followed his orders without hesitation.

The interior lights turned on in a bright burst. I shielded my eyes and tried to adjust by blinking rapidly.

Logan came into view as we entered the lobby.

He stood flanked by three men in identical black tactical gear. "Annie Murray, we meet again." A smug grin curled at the edges of his mouth. "But it looks like your little charade is up." He shifted his weight to one side and folded his arms across his chest with the confidence of someone who knew he had won.

"This is a big response for me." I didn't comment on how his guards looked like giants towering over him. I had a feeling that might set him off even more.

Liam stumbled into the lobby at that moment, secured by two more guards. "Sorry, you okay?" he mouthed.

I nodded.

"Did you find your glasses?" Logan gave me a challenging stare and then directed his rage at Liam. "Since when did you need a friend to help you find a pair of glasses? You pitched yourself as a stellar investigator during our little session earlier today. I find it odd that you believe you can track down missing persons if you need assistance with an errand."

I could practically see the heat radiating off Liam in angry waves. He stood tall and rigid, puffing out his chest like he was gearing up for a fight.

Not that I blamed him. It was taking every ounce of self-control not to race up to Logan and punch him hard in the gut.

But I was holding the very evidence we needed to inflict much more pain. A lifetime behind bars sounded like the perfect revenge to me.

We needed to keep him talking. We needed to buy time.

"What are you really doing? Why are you sneaking into my building in the middle of the night?" Logan crossed his arms over his chest, puffing out his taut muscles to make himself look bigger.

"Was I sneaking?" I asked with fake sincerity. "I showed the security guard my credentials. I used my key card to enter the building. I wouldn't describe that as sneaking. It was hardly a secret."

Logan glared at me and whispered something to his bodyguards. "We're done playing your little game. You're going to hand over whatever you're hiding under your arm, and then my associates will escort you and your friend somewhere more secluded and private."

"That's not necessary," Liam said, shifting his weight to one side and attempting to move closer to Logan, but the guards held him back. "Annie and I were just leaving, right, Annie?"

"It's not a choice." Logan cackled. "Everyone here understands the implications of what has occurred. I'm done playing these little games. You will give me whatever you found, one way or the other. It's non-negotiable. Then we'll figure out what's next for the two of you."

I perfectly understood the implication. He intended to kill us, just like he'd killed Scarlet and forced Natalie into hiding.

"Why did you kill her? You didn't need to kill Scarlet. Why?" I noticed his entire body tense. "I know it was you. In some ways, I've known it all along. I should have realized it after my meeting with Mark. You sent him, didn't you? Has he been working for you all these years remotely on the East Coast? I have to credit you with covering your bases, and if it hadn't been for a minor slipup, I might have believed his story."

"What do you mean slipup?" He frowned like he was missing something and couldn't catch up.

I concealed a smile. This was good. I was betting he was enough of a narcissist and egomaniac that he would want to hear every detail before he disposed of me.

I locked eyes with him, my gaze unwavering and sharp, matching the steel in his. "His Tesla."

"What are you talking about?" He glanced from one guard to the other as if they knew something he didn't.

"He tried to run me off the road, and he was nearly successful, but then he made an error at dinner when he asked me where he could charge his Tesla."

A brief flash of anger crossed his face. His nostrils flared as he clenched his jaw.

Was he making a mental note to "take care of" Mark when he was done with us?

"And Elspeth? I assume you sent her, too?" I had to keep him talking, and I had to hit the record button on my phone. I didn't break eye contact as I slipped my hand into my pocket. "Why did you need to kill Scarlet, though? You could have let her go. You could have paid her off. There were so many other options."

He balled his hands into fists, the tension rippling through him. He looked away for a moment before meeting my gaze. "She was too persistent," he said, his voice low and brittle like it was about to crack. "She couldn't let it go." A flicker of something—anger, regret, or maybe just resolve—sparked in his eyes. "She had to die."

My knees wanted to buckle. I wanted to fall to the floor. There it was—the confession I had been waiting for.

But was it too late?

Logan raised his right hand and waved his guards forward. "Looks like your fate is similar, Ms. Murray. You should have taken a lesson from your friend and learned when to let go."

TWENTY-NINE

The distant wail of sirens gave me a glimmer of hope, but I wasn't out of the woods yet. I tightened my grip on the evidence, my mind still spinning over Scarlet's hidden message.

There was a thud.

A grunt.

The sound of a struggle.

I froze.

The noise had come from outside.

Someone was here.

The sirens grew louder, rising in urgency.

Were they coming for us?

A sharp crash echoed outside, like a door opened or a chair knocked over hastily. Then a familiar voice shouted in a strained, commanding tone. "Stop! Hands where I can see them."

There was another thud and a scuffle.

And then—silence.

Logan looked from one guard to the other in sheer terror. "What is that?"

The sirens wailed to a screeching halt in front of the building, followed by the rapid thudding of boots closing in. The police were almost here.

I let out a breath as Logan tried to bolt.

Everything happened in a blur. There was a struggle and flashing lights and sirens, guns drawn. The police surrounded us, shouting orders to each other, Logan, and his allies. Everything sounded muffled, like my ears were stuffed with cotton balls.

I felt like I was in a dream. Or maybe more like a waking nightmare.

I couldn't make sense of what I was seeing.

I blinked hard, trying to clear the spots from my vision.

Detective Greene took control of the situation, directing a team of police officers to arrest Logan and his bodyguards.

"It's okay, Annie, you can get up." Liam was above me, reaching for my hand. He caressed it tenderly as he hoisted me to my feet. "We're good."

I blinked rapidly again, my eyes landing on the hazy outlines of Fletcher and Pri, who ran through the front doors.

"Fletcher? Pri?" I raced to hug them both. "I don't understand. You called Detective Greene?"

Pri nudged Fletcher in the waist. "Tell her."

"Tell me what?" I blocked out the frenzy of activity around us, still clutching the documents Natalie had hidden under my arm.

"That was my errand," Fletcher said with a touch of pride. "A backup plan to the backup plan. As Sherlock says, 'Your education never ends, Watson. It's a series of lessons with the greatest for last.'"

"You're quoting Sherlock? Now?" I groaned, throwing my hands up.

"Of course." He rolled his eyes with a little winning smirk and continued unfazed. "Once I heard Serena had been arrested for Fox's murder, I realized there was no point in hanging around Victor's meetup. It wasn't my scene anyway. Just a bunch of tech bros trying to one-up each other. Something good came out of it. It sounds like Victor and Theo are going to partner together on a new and improved version of the Headset. I told them about Laurel's grandson. He may end up with an internship after all."

I pulled my glasses from my purse and put them on. The room suddenly came into sharper focus. Now, I needed my mind to catch up. "What about Theo—did he say why he kept changing his story?"

"He admitted he was petrified Detective Greene would arrest him once she examined his financial records and realized how much money he spent on the launch party. He said he'd read enough fiction to know that the police always follow the money trail. The pro is that he and Victor and potentially Laurel's grandson all share a common interest and seem to be serious about teaming up."

That was good news. I was relieved, although not surprised in the slightest, to hear that Fletcher had pieced together the loose ends with Fox's murder, but I was also singularly focused on Logan and how in the world Detective Greene was here. I blinked again, trying to get my bearings.

Pri patted his wrist twice. "You're losing her, my guy. Stick to the plot."

Fletcher cleared his throat and nodded apologetically. "Yes, of course, you're probably in shock. My stakeout partner and I made an executive decision, along with Liam, before you ventured out this evening. We figured it wouldn't hurt to have the local authorities looped in and on our side. There was technically nothing illegal about our plan. You were rightfully employed by Silicon Summit Partners. It's not as if you broke into the building. I made that crystal clear."

I wasn't worried about technicalities at this point, but I bobbed my head, encouraging Fletcher to continue.

"We gave Detective Greene an overview of Scarlet's cold case and explained we'd had a tip from a reputable source that there was evidence in the building. She agreed to be on standby tonight. I thought it was better than calling 911 if necessary. There would be so much explaining to do, and I didn't want to waste an extra minute if you and Liam were in danger."

"It turns out we made the right call." Pri beamed at him, clapping him on the back like he'd just won the Super Bowl. "This guy, right?"

I leaned in to kiss Fletcher on the cheek. "Thank you."

"You gave me a scare, Annie." He clutched his chest. "When I saw those SUVs zooming down the driveway, I called Detective Greene immediately, but then I was worried they wouldn't get here in time."

"But they did. Well done." I removed the envelope from under my arm and pulled the three of them in for a group hug. "We did it." Tears spilled from my eyes and splattered onto the paper. "I couldn't have done it without you. Thank you."

We swayed with our arms around each other for a few minutes. I let the tears flow—these were welcome tears, tears of grief and the formative years I'd shared with Scarlet, tears of relief that Liam and I and all of the people I loved now were safe, and tears of closure. A case that had haunted me for a decade was finally coming to an end. And we had done it. Justice would be done. With the help of the documents Natalie had gathered all those years ago, Logan would be tried before a jury of his peers. I had every confidence that no matter how much money he spent on expensive lawyers and his defense, he would be convicted and spend the remainder of his life behind bars.

It was time for me to make a major life shift, too, but in a very different direction.

My most important case was closed. I was surrounded by friends who had become family. I was brimming with new ideas and unshakable enthusiasm for the future of the Secret Bookcase. And I, Annie Murray, was a private investigator. There were plenty of other cold cases and mysteries out there waiting for me, and Fletcher and I had proven, beyond a shadow of a doubt, that the Novel Detectives weren't just up for the challenge—we were the perfect pair for the job.

A contented feeling started to build as I brushed tears away with my sleeve. Somewhere out there, a new mystery was already beginning to take shape, and I couldn't wait to dive into the next chapter of my own story.

EPILOGUE

A few weeks later, I scrambled over stacked boxes labeled for donations and to be shelved in the bookstore. Fletcher and I had made slow but steady progress gutting one of the storage rooms upstairs to become the new home of the Novel Detectives. There was still plenty to do, as was evident by the shafts of light filtering in through the arched windows and highlighting the layers of dust and piles of clutter that remained. They would have to wait for another day. I was due downstairs.

I brushed off my skirt and tucked my hair behind my ears, hearing Fletcher calling for me. "Annie, Annie, are you coming? Everyone's here." His voice echoed down the empty hallway.

"Yes!" I replied, hurrying down the corridor. "I lost track of time. On my way." I stopped briefly to grab my cardigan and a sealed envelope that I had hidden away in our shared office for tonight. I clutched it to my chest as I headed for the stairs. I couldn't wait to reveal its contents.

Downstairs, the Secret Bookcase was empty. Customers had long gone home as the light faded into a soft purple, and the tiniest sparkle of stars began to erupt in the night sky. Fletcher paced in front of our newest book display—collections of titles and bookish treasures we'd brought back with us from the convention. "I thought I was going to have to come wrangle you away from your relentless organization. Everyone's on the Terrace." He shot his thumb in that direction. "You can't miss your own party."

"It's your party, too, my friend." I looped my arm through his, tucking the envelope tight in my free hand. "You ready for this?"

"Absolutely. Never more ready." He scoffed as if disappointed I would even suggest otherwise.

"Everything's changing," I said, feeling a swell of happy tears threaten. I blinked them away.

"For the better, though, right?" Fletcher paused and studied me. "This is a good thing."

"The best." I leaned into his shoulder. "I'm beyond grateful, and I'm ready to celebrate. It's just strange to have Scarlet's death in my rearview mirror now. For so long, her death was out there in front of me, elusive and with no possible end in sight. With Logan's arrest, it's been like a whole piece of me has opened up. It's weird, but it's good," I assured him with a little squeeze as we stepped out onto the Terrace and were greeted by cheers.

"There they are, my Novel Detectives." Hal beamed, holding up a fluted champagne glass. Heat crept up my cheeks as Hal handed me a glass of the bubbly champagne. "A toast to our Annie and Fletcher."

Pri, Liam, Penny, and Caroline raised their glasses in response. "Cheers!"

I took a sip, catching Liam's eye through the sparkling crystal goblet. His eyes danced with adoration. It took my breath away and sent a fluttery round of shivers through my body, which I knew wasn't from the temperature outside. A warmth settled over the Terrace thanks partly to the blazing firepit and the dozens of luminaries lining the brick patio. He brushed a strand of hair from his forehead and smiled seductively before lifting his glass to his lips.

"To the Novel Detectives," Hal said, holding his glass higher. "And to Annie's dear friend Scarlet, may she rest easy now."

Hot tears streaked down my cheeks. My bottom lip trembled as I placed my hand on my heart and savored the moment, surrounded by friends, the people I loved most in the world, honoring my first friend. Ironically, Scarlet had brought us all together. It was as if she had gathered her perfect team, intertwining our paths and leaving her indelible mark on each of us. She was here with us, too. I could feel her energy and picture her traipsing through the garden pathways backlit by a symphony of stars running wild and free as she was always meant to be. Solving her murder would never fill the void of her loss, but it patched the hole, weaving the broken pieces of me back together like a tapestry.

I wiped tears from my cheeks and sucked in a wobbly breath through my nose. "Thanks, everyone. None of this could have happened without you."

"Obviously," Pri said, rolling her eyes before playfully flashing a wink, effortlessly cutting through the emotional moment with her usual charm.

Tonight had Pri's touch everywhere. Her brushstrokes were in the pretty pastel lanterns hanging in the trees and on the food table near the firepit. It was draped with swatches of fabric and loaded with platters, tiered cake stands, pitchers, and bouquets of sweet peas and sunflowers snipped from the garden.

"This is for you and Fletcher," she continued, pointing to the mouthwatering display. "We all wanted to do something special for you. It's a group effort. Everyone contributed a favorite dish. Come check it out."

Liam waited for me and caught my hand, gently massaging my thumb and hanging back from the group for a minute. "How you doing, Murray?" His voice was husky and thick with emotion.

"Good. Really good." I bobbed my head, realizing how much I believed it. "It's finally starting to feel real. It's over. It's like I can let her go and carry her with me at the same time, if that makes sense."

"Absolutely." He caressed my hand gently, listening with his whole body. He smelled like rosemary and peppermint. His arms were slightly bronzed from the July sun, making him look like one of the Greek statues in the gardens.

"I also feel like the Novel Detectives is a way to pay tribute to her. She gets to live on a little in everything I touch."

He leaned down, his lips brushing the top of my head, and whispered, "One of the many reasons I love you, Annie."

Happiness radiated through every cell. I stood on my tiptoes to kiss him. His lips were soft and tender. I could have gotten lost in the kiss forever, but Pri's teasing voice pulled us both back into reality.

"Okay, you two lovebirds, break it up. The food's getting cold."

Liam chuckled and wrapped his arm around my shoulder. "Your adoring fans await."

I laughed as we strolled to the table together. There were tea cakes dipped in pastel sugar icing and finished with edible flowers, spring rolls, fruit and cheese kabobs, pesto pasta with heirloom tomatoes, crusty bread with dips, and a grilled pork loin. "This is fantastic. You outdid yourselves, but everything is too pretty to eat."

Penny waved off the thought. She looked stunning, as always, in a halter dress and strappy sandals. "As they say, we eat with our eyes first, so please dig in."

I loaded my plate and cozied up in front of the fire. Somehow, my champagne glass was full again. The effervescent bubbles hit my tongue like fizzy candy. We gathered in a circle, enjoying the midsummer feast under the moonlight, sharing stories, and talking about our plans for the future.

Before dessert, I retrieved the envelope I'd brought from upstairs and clinked my spoon against my glass. "Are you all ready for some news?" I dangled the envelope in front of them and rounded my lips into a circle, drawing out the moment.

"Do we have beg, Annie?" Fletcher scowled.

"Maybe." I gave him a sheepish grin before peeling the envelope open and removing a creamy certificate. "Without further ado, look what arrived—our business license. The Novel Detectives is officially recognized by the great state of California and open for business."

Everyone whooped and cheered.

I passed around the certificate.

A text dinged. It was from Dr. Caldwell.

> Sorry I can't be there to celebrate with you tonight. Duty calls. Please know how incredibly impressed I am with your efforts. Scarlet's family and the many people impacted by her death—most importantly you—all have a touch more peace now. I realize professors aren't supposed to have favorites, but you've always been special, Annie. Congratulations on Novel Detectives. I'll be eager to collaborate with you and Fletcher.

I clutched my phone to my chest, letting the warmth of her words sink in.

People refilled their plates with tea cakes and chocolates. Caroline pulled me aside as I poured a cup of chamomile, caramel, and ginger tea and helped myself to another of Pri's melt-in-your-mouth tea cakes. "Annie, I just want you to know how pleased Hal is that you and Fletcher are continuing what he started at the Secret Bookcase. It's been wonderful to see him relax a bit, all while beaming like a proud parent."

"We feel the same," I replied, adding a splash of cream and a touch of honey to my tea.

She snuck a glance at Hal, who was wrapped up in a conversation with Pri and Penny about Redwood Grove's harvest season. "Listen, I may have a case for you. I'd appreciate it if you didn't mention anything to Hal, but let's chat once you and Fletcher are ready, okay?"

"Sure." I was intrigued and tempted to ask her more, but she scooted back over to Hal, linking her arm through his and joining the conversation. They made a striking couple—Caroline with her long, white hair and softly chiseled features and Hal with his inviting smile and solid stance. He took off his cardigan and wrapped it around her shoulders.

I lingered just for an extra beat, watching my friends laughing around the glowing fire. This was the definition of happiness. This was where I was meant to be.

"Thanks, Scarlet," I whispered as I cradled my teacup and made my way to the circle, slipping in next to Liam and centering into a deep gratitude for everything ahead.

A LETTER FROM THE AUTHOR

I can't thank you enough for coming along on Annie's journey! It's been such a delight to write this series and escape into the cozy world of Redwood Grove and the Secret Bookcase. I hope you've enjoyed getting to know Annie and her bookish crew and I'm excited that there's more to come with a new spin-off series—The Novel Detectives, which will release in early 2026. If you want to join other readers in hearing all about my new releases and bonus content, you can sign up for my newsletter!

www.stormpublishing.co/ellie-alexander

If you enjoyed this book and could spare a few moments to leave a review, it would mean so much to me. Even a short review can make all the difference in encouraging a reader to discover my books for the first time. Thank you, thank you!

Wow, here we are at the conclusion of the Secret Bookcase Mysteries. Your love, support, and kind words about these stories deeply humble me. I always say that books connect us, and I feel that so much with this series. What started as a glimmer of an idea has turned into a full-fledged series and I had so much fun discovering twists and turns along with Annie as I wrote each installment. Now if we could only bring the Secret Bookcase to life somehow... I mean, an Agatha Christie-inspired bookshop seems like a winning idea.

Thanks again for being part of this journey! I hope we'll

stay in touch. I have so many more stories and ideas that I can't wait to share with you!

Ellie Alexander

elliealexander.co

facebook.com/elliealexanderauthor
instagram.com/ellie_alexander

ACKNOWLEDGEMENTS

I must sincerely thank Tish Bouvier, Lizzie Bailey, Kat Webb, Flo Cho, Jennifer Lewis, Lily Gill, Courtny Bradley, Mary Ann McCoy, Ericka Turnbull, Jennifer Moriarity, Sue Leis, Sharon Redgrave, Andrew Skubisz, Cherri Northcutt, Beth Cole, and Jessica Slavik for the awesome brainstorming suggestions for the conclusion of the Secret Bookcase Mysteries. I loved taking your ideas and fleshing them out in this story. Having such a great team of readers, writers, and friends is absolutely amazing. Thank you for your support and your enthusiasm for Annie!

I know I sound like a broken record, especially if you've been following along since the first book, but I just can't say enough great things about the team at Storm Publishing and my incredible editor, Vicky Blunden. Working with Vicky and the entire team at Storm is truly a collaboration at each step in the process from early cover sketches to line edits, and getting the books connected to readers like you. I'm deeply grateful to have Storm as a publishing partner and looking forward to bringing you more books!

Last but not least, thanks to my family for all the chats and trips to Filoli, Redwood City, Los Altos, and the Santa Cruz Mountains. You've been immensely helpful and beyond supportive. A special shoutout to my husband and son for the invisible ink idea. You never know when those elementary school science projects will come in handy!